PRAISE FOR

THE GHOST IN THE HOUSE
by SARA O'LEARY

"I so loved this deeply moving tale of loss and acceptance. A ghost stuck in her house, haunting her husband and his new family." —Edward Carey, author of *Little*

"Sorrowful, lovely and funny in equal parts, *The Ghost in the House* depicts overwhelming love in heartbreaking counterbalance with an inescapable loneliness." —Lynn Coady, author of *Watching You Without Me*

"Sara O'Leary opens the front of Fay's dollhouse life to examine love and grief as only she can, with a penetrating view of the smallest things that make us eternally loving, endlessly lonely, and forever indelibly ourselves." —Marina Endicott, author of *The Difference*

"*The Ghost in the House* is a beautiful reverie on how we live and love, a dream of a novel that left me stealing furtive glances at my loved ones, willing myself to appreciate them more and tell them so while we're all still here. If you've lost someone you love, or wondered what it will feel like when it happens, O'Leary's ghost will haunt you—in the best way." —Jessica Francis Kane, author of *Rules for Visiting*

"A thirty-something ghost yearning for her life, a teenage girl toying with ending hers. Can they help each other to move on? This is the extraordinary premise of Sara O'Leary's *The Ghost in the House*, a novel written with such aching delicacy it will haunt you long after you've turned the final page." —Esta Spalding, author of the Fitzgerald-Trout series

"Sara O'Leary's *The Ghost in the House*, riven by ambiguities and dissolutions, is a story of both love and profound solitude. Piercing, disorienting and tender." —Madeleine Thien, author of *Do Not Say We Have Nothing*

THE
GHOST
IN
THE
HOUSE

THE GHOST IN THE HOUSE

Sara O'Leary

DOUBLEDAY CANADA

Doubleday Canada and colophon are registered trademarks of
Penguin Random House Canada Limited

Library and Archives Canada Cataloguing in Publication

Title: The ghost in the house / Sara O'Leary.
Names: O'Leary, Sara, author.
Identifiers: Canadiana (print) 20179049151 | Canadiana (ebook) 2017904916X |
ISBN 9780385686259 (softcover) | ISBN 9780385686266 (EPUB)
Classification: LCC PS8579.L293 G46 2020 | DDC C813/.54—dc23

Cover and book design: Kelly Hill
Cover images: (silhouette) msan10; (pattern) ba888, both Getty Images

Printed and bound in Canada

Published in Canada by Doubleday Canada,
a division of Penguin Random House Canada Limited

www.penguinrandomhouse.ca

10 9 8 7 6 5 4 3 2 1

Penguin
Random House
DOUBLEDAY CANADA

For the ones I love—trusting that they already know.

CHAPTER ONE

IN THE MIDDLE of my life I find myself alone in a dark room. I am lying on top of the piano. I must have been drinking, and if I was drinking I may have been singing. Never a good idea. Did I black out? The house is silent. Am I alone?

"Alec," I call. I want him to come and help me down. I want him to tell me what I'm doing here. I want him.

But Alec fails to appear. Shaking, I crawl down from the piano and look around. It's night. Late. That bit when it's almost morning. And instead of being tucked up in my own bed I'm waking up in the living room wearing nothing but a white shirt belonging to Alec.

"Pull yourself together, Fay," I say out loud. This is something my mother used to say to me, and I would picture myself like an old-fashioned doll with loosely strung limbs, glassy eyes wobbly in my poor little head. Pull yourself together.

I need to find Alec. I call out his name as loudly as I can, but the air absorbs the sound. It's like a reverse echo. I do it once more and the same thing happens and then I'm too frightened to try a third time.

I will have to go and find him. I walk through the open French doors and step into a swallowing fog.

The next thing I know I'm standing at the top of the stairs.

I look down at a little rectangle of light where the streetlamp shines through the window in the front door—a cross in the middle where the four panes meet. X marks the spot. How have I never noticed that before? I glance behind me, toward our bedroom. Why is the door closed? It's never closed. Then I look down the hall to where the stairs lead up to the attic and see a shadow moving stealthily toward me.

"Alec?"

The shadow pauses. It has a shape but no features.

I hold still. I am dreaming. Perhaps if I wait then I'll wake and be back in my own bed. I try to imagine Alec's body close to mine . . . the warmth he gives off like a furnace both winter and summer, the smell of his neck, the tickle of his curls against my skin.

Wake up, I tell myself. It's time to wake up.

The shape solidifies into the form of a young girl. She has white-blonde hair and pale eyes and there is something wistful about her.

She sees me. She's saying something but I can't hear her. It's like I am too far away even though she's right there, close enough to touch.

And then everything goes black. I wait and wait but the light doesn't change, and the morning doesn't come.

I think about what Gran used to call the loneliest hour of the night and how I've never really understood what she meant until now.

It's light again. Thank God.

I'm in the kitchen and it's morning and this should feel normal, but it doesn't. The house is empty, but Alec has left a radio playing. There are two dirty plates on the table, one of them with a lone triangle of toast. I try to pick up the toast, but it slips through my fingers. Then I lean close to smell it, but it has no scent. I find that I am unbearably hungry—the way we are as children but hardly ever as adults. I think I might cry I want that bread so much.

I move away from the table and that is when I notice what's coming out of the radio. I had thought it was one of those morning call-in shows. It's something even worse. Voices are being interrupted by other voices: shouting, swearing, pleading.

"Are you there?" one man repeats, while an older woman says: "I don't know where I am."

A child's voice, soft and confused, keeps saying, "Hello?" A heart-breaking question mark at the end.

I put my hand on the radio to switch it off and it sparks and goes dead.

I'm alone in the conservatory. In the one place I would most wish to be were anyone to ask.

The odd thing is that I can't smell the flowers, or the warm fug of damp earth. I look around me and everything is thriving and blooming just as usual.

The girl appears suddenly in the doorway. I'm trapped in the room with her and involuntarily back up. I fight to swallow the rising panic.

"Who are you?" I ask. I pull myself upright.

She is perilously thin and more of a teenager than a child. Her eyes are heavily rimmed in black, but the rest of her face is bare. She's a little Goth Alice. Her lips are pale and chapped. It hurts to look at them.

I cross my arms in front of my chest. I am the adult here.

"What are you doing in my house?"

She laughs joylessly. I can hear her now.

I step back. A void divides us.

We are being haunted, that much seems clear. And this idea, outlandish as it is, is easier to accept than the possibility that a rogue child is roaming around my house.

I try to think of everything I know about ghosts. Hamlet's father. Jacob Marley rattling his chains. Scary movies when I was a kid. Twins holding hands in a corridor. Things coming through the television: "They're here." Gran believed in ghosts but in a matter-of-fact way. Why would you ever be afraid of a ghost? she said. Someone who would never hurt you in life wouldn't think of starting once they're dead.

Though even a poltergeist doesn't explain what is happening.

I don't know this child. I don't know where she has come from or what she wants. And why this haunting *now*? We came to this house nearly fourteen years ago.

And then I seem to be slipping through time, suddenly unanchored.

It has been a long and stressful day. The moving truck from Montreal hasn't arrived with our furniture, although we'd been promised it would be here. It is the sort of thing that would usually drive me mad and yet I am at peace wandering through the empty rooms of our new home. Our things will come or they won't. We're fine. We're home.

We spread all the clothes from our suitcases into a

nest on the bedroom floor and sleep there—skin to skin, exhausted and sated. This is happiness.

How I want to be back there. In that moment.

Sunshine pours in through the window above the kitchen sink. Morning? I can't feel the warmth on my skin. The cedar chairs at the back of the yard where Alec and I like to sit look weathered. Sadly empty.

I can feel the house is empty but even so I stand still for a few moments to listen for sounds. I look at the clock: just after ten. Alec should be at the newspaper. Unless it's the weekend. The last morning I remember clearly was Monday—wasn't it? Or maybe Tuesday. But how many days have I lost since then? There's a calendar on the wall, but for some reason it frightens me. There's something threatening in those neatly squared-off segments of time.

I feel oppressed by the silence.

Where have I been?

Why am I wearing nothing but my string of big black pearls and a rumpled white Oxford shirt of Alec's? I think I went to bed wearing the pearls but am less sure what happened after that.

And a ghost. Did I see a ghost?

I stretch out on the sofa nearest the window and close my eyes to think. I try to pin myself to the sofa, to the room, to the day. I want to be here when Alec comes back from work. I need to talk to him.

I have never felt so alone.

I open my eyes and realize the strangest thing. The walls should be wallpapered. That lovely, dark-blue damask. Instead, they've been painted a colour that can only be described as *greige*.

Someone has been in here and changed things. My overflowing magazine rack has vanished. Our battered burgundy leather Morris chairs are gone. In their stead, a pair of slipcovered wing chairs the colour of the smudge you leave behind when you erase something written in pencil. My dark-red velvet sofa has been replaced with a non-colour one, somewhere between stone and sand. Everything in the room has been made neutral. Neutralized. I feel like I'm in one of those crappy home-redecorating shows where the woman comes in at the end and all she can do is say "Oh my god" and cry.

Alec comes through the front door.

He'll know what's wrong. He'll know how to fix this.

"In here, Alec," I say.

I wait but he doesn't come into the room. Since when does he ignore me? "Alec!" I call again. I can hear him walking down the corridor. Away from me.

I get up to go to him, but as I cross through the door-way I slip into nothingness.

My dollhouse is missing. The one object I would rescue if the house were on fire, and it is nowhere to be seen. The dollhouse sits on the table by the window—that's what the table by the window is for. And then I return to the moment I first saw it.

Alec is watching me and smiling. "Thank you," I say. "No one has ever given me exactly the thing I wanted before I even knew I wanted it."

It is our house made small—about two feet tall. A miniaturized version of the house we are standing in. It's just the kind of dollhouse I might have wished for as a child. I walk all the way around it, marvelling at how I have suddenly become some benign giant.

I crouch to peer through one of the windows. A replica of the large living room window we're currently standing in front of. There's nothing inside the small house but shadows.

"There we are," I say. "I can see us there."

Alec laughs and reaches out his arms for me and the moment shimmers mirage-like, as if we are in both places at once. As he embraces me, I look over his shoulder out the large picture window as though I might see another self, looking in.

I close my eyes and open them again and I am here, and the dollhouse is gone.

Our symbolic home is gone, and there is a large vase filled with white roses in its place. I don't like fresh-cut flowers as a rule. I have never been able to shed the memory of my mother surrounded by the bouquets that were delivered to the house after Dad died. Crying and saying, "If only we could eat lilies."

Something has happened. Somehow I've been standing still, and the world has moved on without me.

I'm in the conservatory. The walls are that beautiful blue that changes with the light. The colour not of a perfect sky but of a shared one. I look out into the backyard.

There are leaves on the ground, the shrubs are flame red. The flower beds bare and dry.

It's June. It should be in full June-bloom out there, and it's not.

There's a piece of yellow notepaper clipped to a fern hanging down from the ceiling. Why? I pull it down and hold it close to my face to read it.

Ghost, it says.

CHAPTER TWO

USUALLY I KNOCK before I go into Alec's study. If the door is closed it means that he's working, and I hate to interrupt his writing. I stop to listen for the sound of his keyboard.

I try to turn the knob and it slips through my hand. Or, to be more accurate, my hand slips through it. Objects have lost their solidity. I concentrate hard, think of the shape of the crystal-faceted doorknob and how it used to feel under my palm. I imagine turning it and find suddenly that I can. The door swings open and I'm rewarded with the sight of Alec there at his desk. I feel a surge of relief.

"Alec," I say, crossing the room. This has all been some kind of nightmare. Everything will be fine now. "Oh, love. I thought—"

He looks straight through me. I wonder how many times I've used that expression without truly understanding how wretched it could feel.

I reach out to touch his shoulder but before I can a shudder runs through his body. I draw my hand back. He looks around the room. His glance passes over me once and then again.

He looks normal. Yet different. His face is leaner—as though the bones have moved forward—and his hair is now greying at the temples. And yet he looks younger too. His hair is longer. It curls over his ears in a way I don't recall ever having seen before. And he's wearing a lilac shirt. Lilac!

But he's still my beautiful man.

He picks up his book. Alec always has a book to hand. He's the most well-read person I know. He used to read me whole chapters at bedtime, and I would fall asleep to the deep rumble of his voice. The timbre both stirring and soothing.

I lie down on the couch and look up at a speck on the ceiling. If I stare long and hard enough maybe I'll become that speck.

Ghost.

———

A light appears at the top of the cellar stairs and I see a silhouette in the doorway.

A laugh. It's not Alec. My spine tingles when I realize it's her.

She creeps down the stairs and turns on the lights and I see that the cellar has changed as much as the upstairs. The walls have been covered with tacked-up batik bedspreads— the kind that looked ridiculously hippie-ish even when I was young. A futon has been pushed into a corner, with an upturned milk crate beside it. On the crate lie an ashtray and an incense burner, and for the first time I'm glad that my sense of smell has been lost.

"Sit down," she says.

I look around. It's the futon or nothing, so I sit on the edge of it. She shimmies her skinny little hindmost backwards until she is pressed back against the wall, and then she pulls her knees up to her chest, wrapping her arms around her shins.

"Can I call you Fay?" she asks.

She knows my name. I nod reluctantly.

"Good," she says. "You can call me Dee." She is speaking in what I imagine she thinks of as a grown-up tone. She's drawn a wobbly black line along her eyelids. She is absurd.

"Why are you dressed like that, Fay?"

I'd kind of forgotten. Being half-naked has been the least of my worries, but now I feel exposed. I pull the shirt closed across my breasts and fumble at the buttons, but they remain undone so I cross my arms.

"I don't know," I say.

She tells me that if I want to ask some questions she will do her best to answer them. An urge to laugh competes with an urge to cry.

"What are you doing in my house?"

Dee makes an impatient little noise.

She's so young. I'd like to know how she died but it's not the sort of thing you ask someone, is it? She's thin to the point of frailty, and I can't help but wonder if she starved herself to death. "How old are you?" I ask instead.

"I'm thirteen." She shifts herself on the futon like she has grown bored with me and is preparing to leave.

Thirteen.

Thirteen years ago, what I lost was just a collection of tissue, a mass. That's what I always told myself. Cells. But now I think about those cells taking shape, becoming a living, growing organism, with a smile that reminds me fleetingly of someone I'd once been.

I search her face for proof.

Try to see Alec. Try to see myself. She has the same Scottish fairness that Gran did. The gold in her green eyes could come from Alec.

I reach out to touch her face, but before I make contact a blue flash passes from my hand.

"Ouch," she says. "You gave me a little shock. I didn't know you could do that." She shivers.

"Neither did I," I whisper. My child. I want nothing more than to take her in my arms, but she is somehow both right there in front of me and beyond my reach.

In another life Alec and I had three children—two close together and then one years later, an unexpected gift. A girl and then a boy and then another girl. When the first was born we were newlyweds—still just getting to know each other—and so the three of us have been together nearly as long as the two of us. Our daughter, our darling first-born, hates us. But we know that this is just a phase and we are prepared to wait it out. Our middle child, the boy, is sad more often than we would like. And as much as we want to see this as something that too will pass, it appears unlikely. He is who he is, and we fear for him. Our last-born is wild and fearless, and she is both the best and worst of us combined. We feel so much for her that we can barely stand to look at her.

We take far too many pictures of them at all their different ages and stages. We are trying to fix them in time. Sometimes we look at pictures from when they were younger and miss them even though they are still here with us. They were each so fiercely themselves at birth that our parenting feels practically irrelevant, as though we are merely here as witnesses.

Sometimes I wake in the night and forget that I have borne children, and then it all comes rushing back to me and I smile into the dark. I can never be as close to anyone as I am to this person who has made these people with me. We are a family—ourselves and larger than ourselves.

This is our other life. The one we never lived.

I need to talk to Alec, to tell him about how the child we lost may have been here in the house with us all along. I can see her. But why now? Has she been waiting for me all this time?

I was twenty-four when I got pregnant. It was over almost before it began. An ectopic pregnancy. Such a strange word. *In the wrong place.*

Termination was the only option. I had the injection rather than the surgery.

Everyone said, "You're young. There's plenty of time." And there was. But then suddenly I was thirty, thirty-five, thirty-seven. And when I think about all that time, all that plenty, I can't be sure where it went.

But that lost pregnancy. Our lost baby. She was no hypothetical child. She was real and then suddenly she wasn't. But what if there is some other reality where that child lived? Where she grew. Where she and I are now together.

Nothing makes any sense. All the rules I thought applied were wrong.

I'm sitting on the stairs and staring at the front door. There is a puddle of late-morning light at my feet and I'm being lulled into a hypnotic state by the motes of dust slow-dancing through the air. I think about the word *suffused*. I am suffused with calm.

Then a woman walks into the foyer from the dining room. She is youngish, thin, blonde—all sharp edges. I've never seen her before.

"Are you there?" she calls out. She doesn't look in my direction.

She's dressed in close-fitting black clothes. Very trim and elegant. She turns her back on me—cool as you like—then opens the hall cupboard and takes out a trench coat. Beige. Definitely not mine.

She turns and calls down the hallway, "I'll be back in a few hours, sweetheart."

She waits, as though expecting an answer, re-adjusts her purse so it's sitting higher on her shoulder. I walk over to where she is standing, looking at herself in the mirror, so that I should be right there in the reflection with her— no reaction. No flicker in those grey eyes. I look and see myself, which is worse than not seeing myself. The woman steps away and I am left staring at my bedraggled reflection. My hand goes up to the pearls around my neck. What has happened to me?

She opens the front door and steps out without a

backward glance. When did I last leave the house? Not since I found myself on the piano.

I can't hear anyone else in the house. That "sweetheart" hangs in the air.

I look at the light streaming through the window in the front door.

I consider the door. Imagine it opening.

I am looking for Dee. I want to tell her that she's safe with me. That no matter what is going on in the house, no matter who that woman was, no matter what's wrong with me, I can look after her. She needs to know she is safe.

I wonder if she's in the cellar and if I can get from the living room to the kitchen and then down there. One doorway, one door and one flight of stairs.

There's a flickering light coming from the bottom of the cellar stairs, and I slowly make my way down toward it. As I turn the corner, I see Dee. She has one of those craft knives with the click-up blades and she is using it to cut not paper but her arm. And that isn't even the most shocking bit: she's bleeding. The ghost girl is flesh and blood.

She's alive.

Now I'm standing in the foyer, and I have the funniest feeling I've forgotten something. That there's somewhere I'm supposed to be. The house is quiet. It's daytime now. The next day?

Then I remember the girl. I saw her, what she was doing. And then I faded. She needed me and I did nothing. I'm suddenly frantic. I only hope I'm not too late.

Not a ghost. Not my child. But a child who needs me.

I wrench open the door to the cellar, hoping to find her there—hoping she's all right. Hoping she's still alive. And then comes the realization that if she is alive then I am the ghost.

There are no stairs and I feel myself begin to fall. Panic builds and I scream but I am a tree alone in the forest. No one hears.

CHAPTER THREE

THE DARKNESS RECEDES and I find myself in the conservatory again, but I'm not alone. Alec is sitting in his chair. Staring into space. I look at him and feel a wave of grief. I want to drop into his lap, nuzzle his neck, inhale his familiar scent. I want him to reach out for me, make a space for me to move into. I stand directly in front of him. Yearn for him to see me. He tilts his head back so that his gaze points upward.

"Look at me," I say.

He closes his eyes.

And then, with a jolt, I remember Dee. The glossy

red beads of blood on her arm. The blankness of her face looking up at me.

When I finally get myself down the cellar steps I find Dee lying on the futon with headphones on. I say her name three times before she opens her eyes.

"Oh," she says, taking off the headphones. "Hey."

She is not my ghost girl. She is not my anything. Still I am so relieved that she is alive.

"Are you okay? I was scared to death."

She laughs.

"It's no joke. Show me."

I make her pull up her sleeve. Pencil-thin lines score her flesh. I'm not sure I've ever seen anything so desperate.

"Why, Dee?"

"Don't worry about it," she says.

I wonder what she would think if she knew I'd mistaken her for a ghost. I suspect she'd be pleased.

I sit beside her and try to work out what I'm supposed to say.

Dee edges away from me. "You're cold," she says.

I wonder if this is true or if she's just trying to distract me.

"Why?" I ask. "Why would you do that to yourself?"

She shrugs and pulls her sleeve back down. "I'm a cutter," she says, like it's some club she belongs to.

She spends several minutes examining the cuffs of her shirt as if she's written answers there to questions she's still waiting to be asked. I watch her and think how badly we are put together.

"You are never, ever, to do that again," I say in the firmest voice I can muster. I am absurd.

Dee rolls her eyes. "Who do you think you are? Do you think you're something just because you were married to the sad widower guy who married my mom?"

It all takes me a moment to grasp. This child now lives in my house with her mother and my husband.

"How did I die?" I ask her. I immediately want to take back the question. I'm frightened. It's not the sort of thing you should hear about yourself. I don't want her to tell me. And yet I do.

"How should I know?"

I look at her. She has pressed her hand against her mouth as though stopping herself from speaking. I think she knows and just isn't saying. It makes me want to shake her.

"Okay, but when. You must know when?"

"Ages ago," she says. "Five years, maybe."

Five years! The world has kept on turning without me for five years. Suddenly my brain is caught in one of those old exam problems: Imagine Fay is travelling on a train going sixty kilometres an hour while Alec is in a car travelling one hundred kilometres per hour. Will they ever arrive anywhere together ever again?

Dee's right. I am nothing here.

———

Alec is alive and I am somehow dead. When we were kids, Mira's grandmother used to stand on the street corner waiting for the bus to heaven. They said she had dementia but now I'm not sure. Now I feel like there was a bus and I missed it.

I am the ghost here, and instead of being in the next life with people who loved me, I am haunting my own house and my husband is living with someone who is not me.

I think of all the squandered days—days we spent apart, days we turned away from each other in anger. If I added them all together and had them to re-live now, how much extra time would that give us? Time to do ordinary things. We were going to get old together. He was going to go bald and I was going to "let myself go" and start wearing kaftans, and it wasn't going to matter because we'd always see each other as the people we were when we met, when we first understood that the days and nights of being alone were at an end. That was the bargain.

That was the future I've lost, but it feels like the past has been taken away from me as well. How long have I been gone? How soon did he replace me? I remember the day I realized that I was done. I wasn't looking anymore. I had found what I wanted. And when I told Alec he said he felt the same. Nothing in my life ever mattered to me the way that mattered. And now I have been replaced?

———

I need to learn to control when and where I fade in and out and I have to talk to Alec. It seems to me that I'm most likely to be alone with him in his study. So I try as hard as I can to visualize myself there: the deep merlot leather psychiatrist's couch, the beautiful saffron swirl in the astrakhan carpet, the pewter tankard full of pens on the desk, the maple shelves filled with row upon row of books.

Instead I find myself in the last place I want to be. I'm in my darkened bedroom, standing at the foot of the bed.

I loved my bed. It was one of the first things I bought for this house after we moved to Vancouver with all our bits and bobs from Montreal. I found it in an antique shop up on Main Street, and I bought it with my first month's pay from my wretched temp job, even though I'd taken the job so we could manage the mortgage. The bed was enormous. Made from iron, which seemed to me to imply stability and longevity, or at the very least something difficult to destroy. It was four-postered and grand. French, the fellow told me. Probably nineteenth-century. It had found its way to this particular part of Vancouver all the way from Paris, perhaps from a home where generations had been born and died—and then somehow the bed had found me. I ordered blue linen sheets and a silk eiderdown. I bought colourful Kantha throws for it. It was like sleeping in a fairy tale illustrated by Dulac. But now my bed has been replaced with something sleeker, more modern.

I am trying not to register that there are two people sleeping side by side. I can't bear to look, and yet I do. A woman's fair head rests on the curve of his upper arm and her hand is on his chest, curled protectively around his heart. They are nude from what I can see. The moonlight makes them look as though they are made of marble. The sheets are tangled around them as if sleep found them unawares. At least she sleeps on the wrong side.

I wonder if he ever wakes surprised that there is someone not me in his bed. I wonder if we're still married in his dreams. If I am still alive there.

Alec used to tell me there was nobody but me for him. And I used to believe him. But now I would tell him otherwise: You like someone to sleep with and you also like someone to wake up with. You like pressing your body so close to another's that your bones knock together. There are lots of things you like. Being alone isn't one of them.

In the early days of our marriage it was all soft-focus romantic talk. All that *a little girl with your eyes, a little boy to play catch with*. Dream children. I don't think either of us believed in them. Not really.

Then I did get pregnant and all of a sudden our conversations were about the next twenty years of our lives. Schools, and daycare or no daycare, and breast is best, and religion, and godparents, and should we make a will, and, yes, of course we should. I worried that we weren't ready. Alec said we would be fine, that babies bring their own love with them. And he was so happy he convinced me into happiness.

We were all set to become a family and then it was just us, still. We started talking about trying for another baby. Perhaps I wasn't ready after all, I told Alec. We've got all the time in the world, I remember saying.

When I was a teenager I was so lonely that sometimes I thought I must have had a twin that died in the womb. Or that I was living in the wrong family or the wrong place or the wrong time. I always felt like other people lived in their bodies and I lived just a hair's breadth to the left of mine. I would always be covered in bruises from walking into the furniture and doorways, like I couldn't quite navigate the body I had found myself in.

It was only after meeting Alec, after loving Alec, that I finally felt that my body was my home.

And so, it was just the two of us. That was enough. As the years went by it seemed to me more and more that we already had everything we needed. We were happy. I think of all the things I meant to do and the things I actually did do. There was the job I took at Ficciones bookstore when I first moved to Montreal. I loved that one, actually. Might have stayed there forever if the bookstore hadn't closed. Most days I sat and read and had occasional conversations with other readers. What could be better? Then we moved back here, and I was thinking about art school but then along came Mira's offer of a job working for her, which was only supposed to be temporary at first. It seemed ludicrous. I was lousy at organising my own house, never mind someone else's. But I loved the clients—all their needs and neuroses, the stories they longed to tell someone, their funny assortments of treasured objects. And so I stayed.

How did I go through my life and make all these decisions without realizing they were decisions? Why did nothing ever feel final? Until now. All my choices have been made. I will never give Alec a child. He will never give one to me. We will never give one life.

———

I'm sitting in the foyer, waiting for a glimpse of Alec.

I hear a woman's voice calling from the kitchen: "Dee! You're going to be late again. I'll drive you, but we need to leave now."

She walks into the foyer and stands in front of the mirror, putting her lipstick on. It's a perfect red, the kind of red you spend your life searching for. She puts her hand up to adjust her hair but it is already perfect. Who is this woman?

And then, her phone rings and I hear her say: "Hi, it's Janet."

Her name is Janet.

"No, Al's not here. He's gone in to the paper," she says. *Al!* I don't think anyone's called him that in his adult life.

And then there is a pause before she says: "No, I haven't left yet. I'm still at home."

Home.

On a July day thirteen years ago, we left our de l'Esplanade apartment as two single people and returned to it married but essentially the same. I kept my name—Fay Turner—it was a good name and it fit me. I had this idea that marriage wouldn't change us, wouldn't change me. I disliked the idea of engagements, of being asked, of being chosen. It felt antiquated and ill-fitting. But I came to realize that I really did like being married. I liked the idea that we had chosen each other. That as improbable as it all might seem, all the days before we met had been leading up to that one day that was the start of our life together.

And then we bought this house in Vancouver, and I felt grown up, married. I was in love with our house. This house that matches the sky on days when it's bright and clear. This house so different from the ugly, squat, squatter of a house we moved into when I was thirteen. That house was a Vancouver Special—that's what they called them, although there was nothing the least bit special about it. It wasn't even all ours. I hated that house. It was only slightly older than I was, but it was rundown and tatty. Cheaply thrown up in a neighbourhood filled with beautiful, solid Craftsman houses.

As a child, I walked past this house many times, and it had always been my favourite. Partly because of the blue paint, but also because of all that the symmetry of its construction implied. I didn't know the people who lived here but I pictured them leading perfect, orderly lives. I would stand on the sidewalk and look up, imagining my future. "I'm going to live there one day," I would tell Mira. Not that either of us really believed it then.

When Alec was first offered the job at the *Sun*, I wasn't sure I was ready to leave the life we had built in Montreal. I was afraid to jinx what we had. But when Mira told me this house was for sale, it felt serendipitous—like it was time to come home.

Alec is sitting on the couch, reading a book and eating a bowl of pistachios. I've never seen him eat pistachios. Maybe I assumed things about him for so long that they became as good as true. Like not eating pistachios. Like not being attracted to blondes. I sit down beside him, and he shudders. I inch away.

I wonder if this is now as close as I will ever get to him.

Why can he not see me when Dee can? If it had to be anyone, it should have been him.

Janet comes in and sits between us on the couch. I can get a good look at her now. She is pretty rather than beautiful. Her features are slightly too regular. Her hair is a pale blonde with streaks of paler blonde. It looks expensive.

She looks nothing like me, and I'm surprised to find that this hurts.

I move nearer to her to see if I can make her shiver, and she does. But then she snuggles into Alec's side and gives—honest to God—a contented sigh. He looks at her in a way that was only ever for me.

I'm back at the piano, although not actually on it this time. I do love this piano. It's a beautiful thing. A Steinway baby grand. Mahogany. I take pleasure in looking at it. I was always going to take lessons but never did. Alec bought me songbooks and I learned to pick out a song or two in a way that would have been admirable if I'd been in grade school but was somewhat underwhelming given I was a grown woman. You have to be patient, he would tell me.

But I couldn't.

I'm listening for the front door to open, signalling Alec's return from work, but instead I hear Dee roaming from room to room and calling my name. This must mean she's the only one in the house.

"Fay," she calls in her thin voice. "Fay, come out and play!" She laughs.

She comes around the corner and sees me sitting at the piano.

"There you are," she says.

"I was waiting for you to get home," I lie.

She sits down beside me on the piano bench. Hammers a key with one finger. "Why do you think you can see me when Alec can't?" I ask, resisting the urge to slap her hand away. My poor piano.

"How should I know?" she says.

I get up, stand at the front window and look out at the street. Think of my child self looking in.

———

Dee and Alec are sitting in the kitchen, eating cinnamon buns. He buys them from the place up the road called Grounds for Coffee. I always thought it was a funny name.

"Don't tell your mother I'm ruining your supper," Alec says.

"I will," she says.

Dee is smiling. She looks like a different child when she is smiling. It's Alec bringing this out in her. He's always had a light he could shine on people. A sort of heightened attentiveness. He would have been a good parent. I'm sad to realize that he's always had this in him. I wonder if the same could have been true of me.

Dee looks up and sees me and her expression changes. She has been caught being happy in spite of herself. She pushes her plate away from her. Alec looks at her with concern.

"I was thinking maybe we could all watch something together later," he says. "You, your mother, me."

"Do you like ghost stories?" Dee asks him.

"Films, you mean?" asks Alec.

I think about a long-ago evening spent curled up in bed, watching that old black-and-white comedy with the crazy medium. What was her name?

"No, I mean do you like real-life ghost stories," she says. I step forward so as better to see Alec's face. "Do you believe people can come back from the dead?" she asks.

"Revenants?" asks Alec.

"No, ghosts. Do you believe in ghosts?"

She looks at Alec. He looks down into his coffee cup as though he might find the answer there.

"What if it can happen? What if the dead can come back?"

Alec is silent.

"Well, what if they could? Would you want her to? Your first wife?"

This makes me reel. *First* wife.

"Dee," he says gently.

"What?" She crosses her arms in front of her. Waits.

"I'm married to your mother now. We're very happy."

He looks closely at her, trying to gauge her reaction. Probably trying to understand where this whole line of questioning has come from.

She looks up at me, raising her eyebrows. "But what if your real wife came back?" I feel a surge of fondness when she says this. I nod approvingly.

"Dee," says Alec. He reaches out and takes her hands in his so that she is forced to look him in the eye. "I am not going anywhere."

I'm in the attic. The madwoman in the attic. I sit down on the bed and look around me. I guess this must be a guest room now. This was the most cluttered room in the house and now there's just a bed and an enormous dresser, and one of those cheval mirrors with a blanket thrown over it. The furniture all looks brand new and a bit hotel-ish.

I've been thinking about those Kübler-Ross stages of dying: anger, denial, bargaining, depression . . . I'm trying to work out where I am so I can tell how far I have to go. I think I'm stuck on anger. Anger that my life has been cut short. All the things I'd been waiting for have been stolen from me. I won't grow old with Alec. We'll never have a child. But there were five, though, in that film *All That Jazz*. Five stages and I can only remember four. Anger, denial, bargaining, depression . . . I search my memory but I just can't remember the fifth.

THE GHOST IN THE HOUSE

I'm standing in the doorway, deciding where to sit. The pub is half empty. I came on a whim, with an hour to kill before my meeting at the gallery on the other side of the street. My eye is drawn to a man on the far side of the room sitting at a table by himself. He's older than me, I think, and he's handsome. There's something distinguished about him, but also a little rugged. His dark curly hair looks like it's trying to escape his head. His beard is dark, reddish, and full. He's reading an old, cloth-bound book. I can see the gold lettering on the cover. *The Gist of Swedenborg.* He has a half-empty pint of Guinness in front of him, the foam clinging to the sides of the glass.

He looks up and catches my eye. He smiles, and I smile back. Is there a word for something like déjà vu, but for a person? A person you don't know but feel you know or must have known. I feel this pressing need to wrap his curls around my fingers. It's a kind of pleasant ache.

There is something about this moment, the way it thrums with energy. I try to look away from him and find that I can't. He mouths the word *hello.* Inclines his head toward the seat across the table from him. I do have an hour to kill, and nothing to lose. I sit at his table, directly across from him. His eyes are clear and hazel. A starburst of gold encircles his pupils.

And then I am here. In the present. And I remember. Not "dying." It wasn't the five stages of dying, it was the five stages of grief. I may have reached bargaining. I just want one more day.

CHAPTER FOUR

DO ALL GHOSTS get trapped in the houses where they
last lived? Have I been here all this time, or was I somewhere else? I suppose home is where I would come, given
the choice. But what happens if your house is demolished?
Is Vancouver now populated by homeless ghosts?

My father would be younger than me now. How
strange. I was thirteen when he died; he was thirty-five. Is
he still in our old house? Did I miss out on seeing him all
those years?

My father was a playwright and my mother an actress.
This was the official version. My mother had stopped acting

when she got pregnant with Vicki, and my father was a sometime landscaper, housepainter and handyman, a jack of all trades and master of none. My mother was certain that my father was going to have some great breakthrough, that all their debts would be paid off and everything would be fine.

Instead, he died, and my mother seemed to go to bed for about a year. And after that, she went through the motions, cleaning houses, providing for Vicki and me however she could. And then, a few years later, caring for her sick mother. It was only after she retired, living in the smallest apartment in the world, filling her time with books and walks, that I realized she was finally happy.

I never thought of her as being brave for living through that death. At the time it felt like something that was happening only to me, my father dead, my mother gone. I resented her. I never thought about her being with him, about her seeing him go. Not until the time I accidentally midwifed a death.

It was the holiday Monday at the start of September. Labour Day. I wasn't supposed to be working. I'd given my cell number to a few of my favourite clients—even though Mira had warned me not to—and Marjorie had called to ask me to tea.

We'd been hired initially by Marjorie's nephew. He'd been in the process of moving her into an apartment, and he'd wanted us to clear all the extra stuff out of her house.

Anything that could be of value, he'd asked us to set aside so it could be appraised. Marjorie knew what was valuable, but she refused to say. The only items she wanted to hold on to were those that had belonged to her son. He died when he was nineteen and she'd never gotten over it. It seemed so sad to me that this boy had lived and died and she was the only one left to remember him. She gave me a photo of him on a motorcycle and I put it in my wallet and kept it there after she was gone. Like I'd inherited the duty of remembering from her.

We were in Marjorie's new, tiny apartment having tea when she died. I'd brought over a Sara Lee pound cake because she had recently told me how much she'd been craving one. I almost hadn't gone to pick it up for her, thinking I'd leave it for next time, but she'd sounded so low on the phone. I went into the kitchen to slice it, and when I got back to the living room Marjorie was slouched in her chair, her chin resting on her chest.

I crouched beside her and slipped my hand into hers. It was cold. Then, suddenly, it gripped mine.

"Marjorie?" I said. "I'm here." Her eyes were glazed and unseeing. Her grip relaxed.

And she was gone. I felt her go. Felt that I was alone.

All I want is to be with Alec.

"I want us to be together," he says. I can feel his breath tickling the little hairs at the back of my neck just before he kisses me there.

"We are together," I say. The two of us have spent all the nights and most of the days of this past week in this single room, keeping out the winter chill by doing things furtively underneath the quilt his grandmother made even though we do not feel the least bit furtive about what we are doing. Last night I woke in the dark and we were holding hands like little children. Like we'd been lost in the woods and then found each other.

Alec has finally gone out for supplies and I have been waiting for his return.

"You know what I mean," he says. I can smell the coffee he has brought home for me and beneath that the sharp bite of the cold outside air and the smell of cigarettes on his clothes. He presses the length of himself up against me through the quilt I am wrapped in. I can smell his own smell underneath all the others he has brought in with him. I sip my too-sweet coffee.

We have been talking about marriage. About children and the future. I've been telling him I'm not ready and he's been telling me that he is ready enough for the both of us.

"Just say yes," he says. "Say yes to everything."

I lift the blanket so that he can snuggle in beside me.

"Why do you have so many clothes on?" I ask. And he laughs.

What I wouldn't give to return to that moment. To stay there.

Dee got sent home from school today. She was caught skipping class and given a three-day suspension.

"I need you to sign my suspension letter," she says.

"Doesn't your mother need to do that?" I am stalling. I don't know whether I can write on paper. I haven't thought to try.

"Yeah, but to get her to sign it I'd have to tell her what happened."

"You should tell her."

"I'm not telling her. Just sign the thing for me."

"I'm not signing it."

She glares at me.

Janet Whyte, she writes in a fat, girlish script.

I wince, like I've fallen on something sharp unexpectedly.

"She took his name?"

"D'uh," says Dee. "They're married."

"Did you change your name?" I ask.

"Why would I? Nothing to do with me."

I kept my own name because I liked it, and used to tease Alec that "Mrs. Whyte" sounded like a character in Clue. But now it seems I left a vacancy for someone else to step into.

Dee is folding up the letter and putting it in her binder. I see she's doodled skulls and flowers all over the inside cover. Half in love with death like all the sweet young romantics.

"They don't have anything in common," she says. "I don't even know what they're doing together."

I know what they're doing together at least some of the time. *Think about something else.*

She holds out a deck of cards to me. I shake my head.

Dee absentmindedly scratches beneath her sleeve.

Apparently Janet doesn't know anything about the cutting. I can't see how this is possible, even if the child does wear her sleeves hanging down over her hands most of the time.

"Why do you do it?"

"Do what?" Dee asks, looking up from her cards. She is laying out a game of solitaire.

"That thing I'm not supposed to mention."

She doesn't say anything for a long time. I wait. Red queen on black king, black nine on red ten.

"I don't know." She pulls down her sleeve and pokes her thumb through a hole in the seam. "Why are you keeping on at me about it?"

Her pointy little shoulders are constantly drawn up in a defensive stance. I wish I could put my hands on them and press down.

I give her what I hope is a reassuring smile.

"But why did you do it to begin with?"

"I thought it might help," she says.

And after that she won't say any more. We both watch the cards as she turns them over and slides them into place, aligning them into something like families.

I'm in the study listening to Alec and Janet talking in the living room. They're making plans.

"I think you should do it," says Janet.

"I'm not old enough," says Alec. "And I'm too old. I'm in-between."

Janet laughs throatily. "Take the money. You're young. Young enough to take a chance."

I wonder if they're offering another buy-out at the newspaper. We had talked about this. About Alec taking the money, walking away from that nine-to-five. All the equity in the house. Freedom. But we never did it. I didn't think it was what Alec wanted.

"It's risky," says Alec.

"Not really. I'm making good money. We'd be fine. You could do what you like. Get away from that toxic atmosphere."

Janet has one of those raspy Lauren Bacall, you-know-how-to-whistle voices, the kind I tried to cultivate as a teenager.

"You could write your book," she says. "Open a book-shop. Do something for you."

"A bookshop?" asks Alec. He sounds bemused but not entirely resistant.

Alec will keep on growing and changing, learning new things and going new places, and I will stay just as I am. I'll become a memory that is tied to one part of his life. His past.

"Do it," says Janet. "Do it, do it."
And then the talking stops.

I'm lying in bed, in our bed, and thinking about how for the first time in my life I am really happy to be living in this body. Strange to think of this hidden potential lurking inside me all these years. I picture a long row of children like Matryoshka dolls diminishing in size. And then I think of myself inside the house like a doll inside a larger doll. I love this house. The life that Alec and I are going to have together—the family we will make together—is all contained in this house. Like potential energy stored up and waiting for us.

"Fay? Where are you? Fay?"

It's Alec's voice. His way of saying my name like he is savouring the shape of it in his mouth. I don't answer right away so he will say it again. I can't wait to tell him about the child we are going to have.

"Fay?" Louder this time.

"Here," I call. "I'm here, Alec. Upstairs."

I can still feel how my body felt then. All that love. All the infinite possibilities.

Dee and I are playing double solitaire. She says handling the cards will be good practice for me. I'll do just about anything for company. Dee may not be mine but right now she's all I have. And because she's acting as though all of this—a girl and a ghost meeting up to play cards—is normal, now I do as well.

"Why do you think only you can see me, Dee? Can you see other ghosts?"

"Yes. I have psychotic powers." She makes a face. Ha, she says. Ha-ha-ha.

I put my cards down. "Be serious."

"Oh, how should I know," says Dee. "Maybe you have to be trying to see a ghost before you can? Otherwise wouldn't they be everywhere? All the time?"

"Were you trying? But you didn't know me. Do you think you brought me back?"

"Of course," she says.

"Have you seen other ghosts?" I ask.

"You're my first."

This house was built nearly a hundred years ago. Can there only be one ghost in a house at a time? Has my arrival evicted some previous spectral tenant? And if so, why did they never make themselves known to me when I was living here? Maybe, as Dee suggests, ghosts only appear to you if want to see them. But there must be something more—otherwise, wouldn't it just be like rush hour on the metro everywhere you went? But maybe you need to be open to the possibility. And Dee was. But what about Alec?

I feel dizzy and look down at the cards in my hand to try and persuade myself this is real. I am really here. Playing cards is oddly relaxing. I used to play gin rummy with Gran when I was small.

"Do you have a grandmother?" I ask.

"Not really," she says.

"Not really?"

"One lives far away, and we never see her because she hates my mom. And the other one is kind of a veggie."

"A vegetarian?"

"No, a vegetable."

When I was a child, my grandmother was the one person I could count on to love me unreservedly. When I was a child, being with her was the safest, warmest place in the world.

"I was thinking," says Dee. "You're kind of like my stepmother, aren't you?"

"What?"

"Well, you were married to my stepfather."

She smiles.

Okay then. I smile. *Okay.*

"Why bring me back?" I ask. "If you really were the one who did?"

"Because . . ." she begins, and then stops.

There is a long pause and I do my best to wait it out.

"Just because."

"Because why?"

She looks at me. Looks away.

"Because you thought it would be cool to talk to dead people? Because you thought Alec wanted me back? Because you were lonely?"

"Yes," she says.

My grandmother once told me that she'd lived with my grandfather nearly fifty years, but that he'd only been alive for twenty-two of them. At the time it didn't mean much to me, but now I understand. I understand too why she refused to sell her house. Why she wouldn't move somewhere more practical. As long as she was still there, so was he.

She was just short of eighty when she died, and I was just short of twenty. Looking back, it seems like I could hardly have been myself I was still so young. Nothing had happened to me yet. I'd never been in love (not really), never been away from home (not for long, and not very far anyhow), and, in truth, I'd never really questioned anything. I was an unbaked version of myself. But she used to look at me like she could see me at every stage of my life, from my babyhood straight on through to the bits that hadn't happened yet. I wish she could have met Alec. I wish he could have heard how the way she said my name was not the same as anyone else. I wish she could have seen that I'd found someone to love me as much as she told me I deserved when I was thirteen, when I was convinced that no one would ever love me at all.

She came to Canada from Scotland when she was young, and I often wonder what she must have imagined during those days and weeks she spent aboard the ship. I asked her once. She said she'd never met anyone who'd been to Canada before she came here because when people left they didn't come back. It must have been like going to the moon, I'd said. No, she told me, it was different. She had seen the moon.

I wish I could speak to someone else who understands that everything good that will ever happen has already happened. If I were with my grandmother again I wouldn't be afraid. I wonder if she is waiting for me on the other side.

CHAPTER FIVE

DEE AND I would not get along as well as we do if I were alive. I wonder if this is as obvious to her as it is to me. I wonder if she knows that I'm only talking to her because I can't talk to Alec. That I hope by sticking around I will find a way to reach him. That she can be of some use to me.

"Dee," I say. "Tell me how you brought me back."

"Do you really want to know?"

I think if I allow myself to look too interested then she will go back to withholding.

"Only if you want to tell me," I say.

"I can do better than that," she says. "I can show you."

She pats the edge of the futon so I will sit beside her. When I do she opens up her phone and holds it up so I can see. *Text Messages from Beyond the Grave.* She taps it and a Ouija board appears. Like the ones we used to fool around with when we were kids.

"It's an app," she says.

What I think but don't say is: How perfectly ridiculous. What I say but don't think is: "That's amazing." She looks pleased. "But why did you choose me?"

"I think you know why. Plus, you are the only dead person I know."

Just when I was getting an inflated sense of my own importance.

"She still loves my dad." Dee's voice sounds younger than usual.

"Did Alec split your parents up?"

"Oh, no," says Dee. "They haven't been together that long."

"How long?"

"Only a year. Maybe a bit more. Anyway, Dad and my mom and I hadn't lived in the same house together since I was small. But that doesn't mean they wouldn't have gotten back together. I know she misses him really. Probably she wants to tell him that she's made a mistake. Probably she wants to ask him to take her back. They were probably too young when they got married. That happens." She speaks with all the wisdom that thirteen can muster. She is pulling the tips of her hair down in front of her eyes to check for split ends. She picks up nail clippers and starts snipping away at individual strands.

I take a good look at her. She is wearing a threadbare Snoopy t-shirt, too small for her and coming apart at the seams. Maybe it's one she wore when her family was intact. I realize that she may have been a happy child once.

Dee has finished with her split ends and I realize she is watching me.

"What?" I say.

"Are you sorry you came back?" she asks. "This must not be how you expected it to be." She seems to be seeing me for the first time. I catch in her little face the realization that I am a person. Was a person.

"No," I say. "I'm not sorry."

I'm alone in the conservatory. Sitting in my chair.

I have my eyes closed. I'm waiting.

"I've brought you tea," he says. "I'll set it down here by your book, shall I?"

"Please," I say. I don't open my eyes. "And thank you." For years he has been bringing me cups of tea with milk in it. I like my tea clear and yet now I drink it this way because he has made it for me.

I hear him settle into the chair beside mine.

"Should we go for a walk?" he asks.

I open my eyes. I look at him and he looks at me and it still feels just the same way it did the first time.

"Yes," I say. "Let's. Later."

I put my feet in his lap, and he rubs his knuckles right into that spot where the nerve runs straight up my spine.

"Bad day at work?" he asks.

"Nothing out of the ordinary," I say. "That's a strange phrase, isn't it?"

"You could always do something else, you know. If you wanted. You can stop anytime. We'll manage. I don't want you doing that job if you don't want to. We'd be all right."

"The mortgage," I say.

"We could sell the house," he says. "It's just a house."

"I love this house," I say. Last year for our anniversary we bought each other a new roof. Who says romance is dead? "You know I love this house."

"And I love you," says Alec. He smiles at me. "Come here," he says. And I do.

I sit in his lap and nuzzle into that spot in his neck that always feels like home to me.

"Shall we go upstairs?" he asks.

And just as I am tingling with anticipation it all vanishes.

I'm alone.

I'm looking for all my things. My computer was up here in the attic and my books and my sewing machine and all my art supplies. All the projects that I never got around to finishing. A load of wooden build-your-own-dollhouse kits. Mini flat-pack furniture. Dollhouse-sized rolls of wallpaper made from photocopied images. Sample pots of paint from Farrow & Ball. Twenty-two blues. A quite decent camera I could never use properly. A storehouse of broken dreams. The last few years I hardly came up here because it reeked of failure. I wonder where it has all gone.

Dee comes in and looks surprised to find me.

"What are you doing in my room?" she asks.

"Your room?" I say, taken aback.

"Alec had it done up without asking when we moved in," Dee says. "Janet said I couldn't say anything because I'd hurt his feelings."

She lies down on her bed with her head at the foot end and gently kicks her feet against the wall. My desk used to sit on this side of the room. There was a cork board right where she is tapping her heels and it's hard not to imagine she is kicking against all my inspiration pins.

"You don't like it?" I look around, registering how little of her personality is imprinted on the room.

She rolls her eyes at me. Points to the open stairwell. "There's no door. How am I supposed to live in a room with no door?"

It's true. It wasn't a big deal for me, but then, I wasn't a teenage girl.

I suppose doing over the room was Alec's way of saying he wanted her here. But there was a perfectly good bedroom at the back of the house on the second floor. They could have asked Dee what she wanted. That's what I would have done. I think.

"Is Alec a good dad?" I ask.

"He's not my dad," says Dee. "I have a dad. Alec is married to Janet. That has nothing to do with me."

"But you like him? Alec?" I can't help asking.

"He's okay, I guess. Kind of boring." She is lying on her back smiling up at the ceiling, and she cuts her eyes sideways to see how I react to this. I do like to see her smile, even if it is at my expense. Alec has always been one of those people who others want to be around. He made me laugh more than I ever had. He wrote little haiku dedicated to parts of my anatomy. He wrote my name in a big heart on his chest with a permanent marker. He sang silly love songs to me in public places. He made me happy.

"When you were my age things were different, right?" asks Dee.

I look at her. Does she think my childhood was all *Anne of Green Gables* or something?

"I mean like when you were alone, you were really alone. Like there was no social media then, right?"

Dee is even more fascinated than I am by the idea of how much things have changed in the five years since I died. She shows me things on the computer and apps on her phone and asks me about television shows. Five years seems like an almost unimaginable passage of time to her. Five years ago she was a child and now she feels like she is someone else entirely. I have to keep reminding myself that she is a teenager. In her reality she could go to school wearing the wrong pair of jeans and suddenly feel like the world is crashing down around her.

Dee is still talking. "...this boy from my school. I mean, I don't know him, but he goes to my school, this boy. And he said that he was going to kill himself."

"What?" I ask. Startled awake.

"It was the middle of the night. He said he was going to take pills. And somebody commented and told him to go ahead and do it and he did."

"What? That's awful."

"I didn't see it; I mean I saw it, but not until after it happened."

"You wouldn't do that, right?" I say.

"What? Take pills or tell somebody else they should take pills?"

"Either," I say.

"Don't be stupid," says Dee.

It's not really an answer.

"Is he okay?"

She shrugs.

"Do you talk to your mother?" I ask.

"About what?"

"Anything."

Dee makes a little noise in the back of her throat.

"You need to talk to somebody. You should tell your mother. About the—" I gesture at my own arms.

Dee makes a noise of dismissal.

You can talk to me, I think of saying. Instead I say: "What do you imagine your life will be like when you're my age?"

"I don't expect to live long," she says. "That's just the feeling I have."

And I can remember that feeling too. Not the feeling that there was all the time in the world, but rather that there was so little time really that it hardly mattered what you did.

"But you wouldn't ever do anything—" I say. I stop. Start again. "You wouldn't ever harm yourself, would you?"

"No. I told you. No," she says. I look at her and try to tell if she's lying.

"Did you and your mom used to get along better?" I ask.

"Did you and *your* mom used to get along?" she says, mimicking me.

Perhaps this is what parenting is actually like. I'm weary. Dee is making me weary.

"Did you?"

"We were a family," she says. "Me and my mom and my dad." Dee looks up and her eyes are shiny.

I've never seen Dee without her heavy black eyeliner, but right now she is fresh from the bath and her skin is flushed and she's beautiful, I realize. She's a beautiful young girl, and it's hard to believe I could have ever taken her for a ghost with all that life pulsing through her. Still, there's something about the fragility of her young wrists that makes me want to weep.

"All that's gone now," she says.

A long time ago I read that novel *Appointment in Samarra*. All I can remember about it is the anecdote at the start about a man who meets death at the marketplace in Baghdad. The man flees to Samarra. Death is waiting and says she was surprised to see him in Baghdad as she had an appointment with him that night in Samarra. That has stayed with me since I read it as a teenager. How neat and how awful it was.

Now I think, what if death had been waiting for me here and I was somewhere else? What if Alec and I had stayed in Montreal and lived a completely other life? Where would I be now? Would we be together still? Would we have a family? Could I still go back? Could I have that life?

"Fay," says Dee and the way she says it makes me think it is not for the first time. "Fay, pay attention."

We are the only ones in the house. I'd been wandering, hoping Alec would appear, before finally coming upstairs to the attic.

"Fay, look," she says. "Look!"

She shows me the red leather satchel that Alec gave me for my last birthday. I love that bag. She takes things out of it one by one and lays them on the bedspread. My string of black pearls is first, coiled and gleaming. I find it hard to look at because it is both lying there and around my neck at the same time.

I pick them up and let them roll back and forth between my hands and remember how they used to warm from being next to the skin and how that made them feel alive. I think of all the sensual pleasures I took for granted for so long and what I would give now for one long kiss from my husband. There used to be more of those in a single day than could be counted, and now I would kill for just one.

"Dead!" Dee says. I look up to see her holding my cell phone. Next she fishes out my wallet—open to my driver's license (how I hated that photo), and my key chain. Then a bottle of Chanel. These familiar things look odd in this context. Did Alec gather these things together after I died? Or were they just left behind? I suddenly think to wonder if he took my library books back.

"How about if I ask you some questions," says Dee. "About your life."

The way she says *life*—a closed set—makes me realize that I now possess a biography with a beginning and an end. I realize that for the time this child has been living in my house, I must have been a strange sort of story to her. A mystery.

She takes a single gold hoop earring out of the bag—one of a pair that I'd loved and had worn constantly until I lost one. Was this the one I lost or the one that remained? She twirls it around on her finger and looks at me, waiting.

"Tell me. What do you think you'll be remembered for?"

This is an awful question. A cruel question. I always expected my life to have more shape to it. Like it would be the second act that would give meaning to everything that had gone before. I mean, I'm only thirty-seven. Does that mean I was middle-aged at nineteen? It definitely means that all the things I was going to figure out before I was forty will never be figured out now. I'll never find out what I'm meant to be when I grow up. I'll never grow up.

Dee waves her hand in front of my face.

"I was an artist," I tell her. "I was working on a big show about dollhouses when I died."

I picture myself standing in a gallery, surrounded by my work. Little houses. One covered in dust, hardened with epoxy. One filled with things made out of other things. One with a giant eye peering through the window.

"Where is it? Your art, I mean?" Dee asks.

"I don't know," I say. "I don't know where it's gone."

I don't tell her that I'd only ever thought about making dollhouses. That I had planned out a whole exhibition of different dollhouses over the last few years. This was after several years where I was obsessed with photographing old photographs and then zooming in until you couldn't tell what you were looking at. Before that it was a printmaking workshop and a class in making stained glass. But I was sure that the dollhouses were going to be my medium. I was excited about this project in a way I never had been before. I'd bought a number of wooden kits and components, and some of that pressed-wood furniture that comes in sheets. I liked the shapes of the pieces on the sheets. All the potential.

Dee reaches into the bag like an amateur magician and pulls out a hairbrush. I can see strands of my hair still caught in the bristles and think about my DNA and how it stops with me.

"Put it away. Please," I say. I can't look at it anymore. It's all so trivial and familiar, and if this is all that's left of me, then I'd rather not know.

"There's more," says Dee. But then she looks at my face and puts everything back into the bag and pushes it back under the bed. There is a little worried number 11 forming between her eyebrows. She is too young to know that one day she'll look in the mirror and that line will be there permanently. She is too young to know anything.

I'd like to know where all of my pictures have gone, the family photos that hung along the stairwell.

In the cupboard of Alec's study, I find a stack of neat white banker's boxes. On the lines marked "Contents," Alec has written KEEP. I lift the lid off one box and, sure enough, there are my photos, still in their frames and wrapped up in tissue paper.

It's the tissue paper that gets to me. The idea of Alec planning this. Buying the boxes at the stationery store and bringing them home. Going back out to buy the tissue paper he wouldn't have thought of on the first trip. Sitting alone in this room and wrapping up my past.

It doesn't take me long to find the photo from our wedding day because it is right on top. It's a terrible photo. We are slightly blurred and looking at each other instead of the photographer. Above our heads is a sign listing the price of gas at the station next to the restaurant we were going to. It doesn't look like anybody's idea of a wedding photo. I couldn't love it more.

I sit down at his desk. The pen feels unwieldy, but I manage. I write what I said to him the first morning we woke up together in this house.

Hello, my life.

I place the note on his desk, underneath the photo of the two of us. And then I go.

———

I am waiting patiently when Alec comes into the study. He spots the items I've left for him. He walks over to the desk and picks up the note. I see the confusion on his face as he reads it. And then he breaks. That's the only way to describe what happens. He breaks wide open and a sound comes out of him like an animal in pain. He folds in the middle as though he's been struck.

When Alec and I first moved in together there was a period when it was a running joke to be surprised to find the other person there when you came home from somewhere. Like you'd found a stranger in your house. Goldilocks sleeping in your bed. Part of the game was pretending to be angry or frightened or just unhappy about this sudden other taking possession of your home. And underlying all that, of course, was a nearly uncontainable happiness. We had found each other. Here we were.

It was that joy of discovery that I was hoping for now and instead I have provoked its direct opposite.

When I come back I find myself in the kitchen. It's night. The same night? I am bathed in misery. I sit and gaze at a crystal bowl in the middle of the table, full of fake-looking pomegranates. Mind you, even real pomegranates look fake, so it's hard to tell. I reach and pick one up. Throw it across the room to see if it smashes. It bounces. I pick up another and do the same. It lands in the sink and clatters all the dishes sitting in the rack. A third hits the top of the fridge and then rattles down into the dead zone behind it.

Almost instinctively I raise the bowl above my head and smash it to the ground.

The hall light snaps on and I hear two voices on the stairs.

When Alec comes into the room he has one arm thrown protectively behind him. Signalling to Janet to stay back.

I'm a threat.

I wait for him to say something to me, to look at me, to react. But he doesn't.

"There's no one here," he says. "Go check on Dee. I'll clean this up."

Alec turns to Janet. She's wearing an apricot silk nightgown that looks like something out of a glamourous old film.

I look at the shards of broken glass on the ceramic tile floor and feel like I could shatter as easily.

Alec sighs as he goes to fetch the broom and the dustpan. He looks tired and I feel guilty for having woken him, for having caused this commotion. He looks around the room and I feel his eyes pass over me. Did he pause?

Janet comes back down the stairs a few minutes later.

"She's in her bed, Al. Sound asleep. It couldn't have been her."

Alec dumps the contents of the dustpan into the garbage under the sink. He looks around the room, and I see his hand go up to cradle the nape of his neck like it does when he is uneasy.

"Nothing to worry about," he says. "It must have been the wind."

Then I'm forced to watch the two of them go up the stairs together. Alec's hand just below the small of her back, dark against the pale silk.

That hand, more familiar to me than my own, resting on a body that is not mine.

CHAPTER SIX

I'M LYING ON the psychiatrist's couch in Alec's study, thinking about Alec's hands and what I would give to feel them on me again. I'm so busy not thinking about the fact that he is upstairs with a woman that is not me that I don't hear the door open.

Alec walks into the room.

I stand up wanting to go to him but I'm frozen in my uncertainty.

And then, quite shockingly, he looks at me. His eyes meet mine and I feel the same charge I felt the day we met. "Fay?" he says.

He sees me. I veer toward the ecstatic and then am brought back to earth. He is shaking his head at me. There is no joy on his face.

"This isn't possible," he says. "You can't be here."

"I'm here," I say.

"I . . ." He shakes his head again. He does this when I am saying something he doesn't want to hear. He always has.

"I don't understand. It doesn't make sense."

I step toward him and then stop because he looks afraid of me. "It's me, Alec."

"This isn't real. You can't be real." He's staring at me like I'm a stranger. The corners of his mouth go up and then down again. Alec once told me that he believed that when we died that we just went out like a light and that was it. He's going to have to re-think all that now.

"Alec," I say. "It's me."

"I can't . . ." He's in the doorway now. He's looking everywhere but at me. "I can't do this," he says, and then he's gone. He's gone, but I'm still here.

I find him in the conservatory, sitting with his head in his hands. I sit down in the chair next to him and wait. He looks at me like I'm something that terrifies him. He looks at me like I'm a ghost. Sorrow rushes through me and I'm jolted by it—the almost physical ache—and I wonder if I'm feeling what he feels.

"Oh god, Fay," he says.

"Aren't you happy to see me?" I try to make my tone light. I try not to let him know that he is breaking my heart.

"This can't be happening. I feel like I'm going mad again."

"What do you mean again?" I ask. "Has this happened before?"

"Not exactly," says Alec. "No. It was more like . . ." He pauses, rubs the space between his eyebrows. "It was more like I thought you could hear me if I talked to you. After it happened, I used to sit in here and have long, one-sided conversations. After you—" He stops. Swallows hard. Gets up and turns his back on me.

"That was you," he says. "The note. The broken dish."

"Yes."

"It was you. It is you?"

"It's me."

"Why were you wearing my shirt?" he asks.

"Why *am* I wearing your shirt," I correct. "You might as well ask me who's on first."

"You don't know?" he asks.

I shake my head.

Here's something that you never think about when you get dressed each day. Whatever you put on could be what you will be wearing when you die. If I'd known I was going to die that day maybe I would have put on the new pewter-grey, fitted dress with real steel woven into the fibres. It would have been the perfect dress to die in . . . beautiful and elegant. Or I could have put on that kimono Alec had bought for me . . . the one with the cabinet of curiosities on the front and the swan on the back. I could have swanned around in the afterlife wearing that. Ghosts in movies are always wearing something swishy.

"And now you're back."

Then he looks at me and it's almost more than I can bear. He reaches out his hand but just before he touches my arm a blue spark travels the gap between us.

"What was that?"

"I don't think you're supposed to touch me. Or I'm not supposed to touch you. I'm not sure which. I didn't get a manual. *The Emigrant's Guide to the Afterlife.*" I pause, as my joke provokes an expression of annoyance. "This is all new to me too," I say quietly.

Alec looks down at his fingertips as though expecting them to be charred.

"You were gone, Fay." He draws a ragged breath. "It's funny how they say *till death us do part*, but you never really think about what that means, do you? You don't think it will happen."

I try again to imagine what it would be like if I had lost him. If I had lived and Alec had died. When I was alive, I imagined it a hundred different times and a hundred different ways. In the beginning—when we were new—it was a sort of delicious agony. Like probing the spot where a tooth had been pulled.

"I know," I say. "I'm sorry." *Sorry for your loss* echoes around in my head. *Don't say it. Don't.* "Sorry for your loss."

A moment of silence stretched long and taut. Then he laughs. His laugh is warm and deep and if I could take up residence in it I would.

"Only you," he says.

We stare at each other for a while. There's nothing to say. There's too much to say.

"Alec," I say, finally. "What happened to me?"

"What do you mean?"

"I mean was I in an accident? Did someone kill me?"

I've been thinking that this must be what happened. There must have been a quick and violent death for my spirit to get left behind this way. I cringe a little at the word *spirit*. I was never clear in my own mind about what happened to us when we died—where we went or what we became. But I always knew that there had to be something more.

"Nobody killed you," says Alec. "You just—" He stops. I see tears coming to his eyes and he blinks them back rapidly.

"You just died," he says.

I just died.

It is almost morning. We are back in Alec's study. He is stretched out on the psychiatrist's couch and I am sitting on the floor watching him fight sleep and lose.

Janet knocks on the study door and in the moment before it opens, Alec sits up and looks around. He sees me and makes a shooing gesture at me with his hands.

Janet puts her head around the door. "Al?" she says tentatively.

"Al?" I say, mimicking her throaty voice.

"Oh god," he says.

Janet comes all the way into the room now.

"What's going on?" she says.

"Tell her," I say. "Tell her that she is surplus to requirements."

He glares at me.

He looks at her and I can see his mind turning over and over.

"Not now," he says.

"Are you okay, sweetheart?" she asks.

I echo her again. I'm being childish. I know I'm being childish.

"Stop it!" says Alec. His voice is harsh. Janet and I both involuntarily take a step back.

"What's going on?" she asks. Concerned where I'd have been annoyed. "I'm worried about you. Did something happen? Al?"

Janet crouches with her face up close to Alec's. To see them so close infuriates me.

"No," says Alec. "Thanks, though. Head. Headache. Brutal. Couldn't sleep."

He looks into her face and I can see what all this is costing him. I can see that he doesn't want to hurt her.

"Let's go into the living room," he says. He doesn't bother trying to offer a reason why. Just gets up and walks to the door, all the while quite deliberately not looking at me.

I could follow if I really wanted to. Surely he knows that. I wait for him to come back to me. I wait and I wait.

I am alone in Alec's study. I browse the bookshelves and hum a little tune to myself. Pretend that it is just an ordinary day. I look for the novel I was in the middle of reading. Not really Alec's kind of thing. Crime fiction. Denise Mina. It was the third of a trilogy and it is unsatisfying to have to leave it unfinished. Not to know how it ends.

I pull down a copy of Emily Dickinson's poems. I open it up and there is my name, written in green ink with my self-consciously confident twenty-something hand. I bought this book when I was still in university, at an age when I thought people would find me interesting if they saw me reading an interesting book. When I flip through the pages it falls to the most obvious of all places: "Because I would not stop for death . . ."

Then I hear Alec and Janet out in the hallway.

"Are you sure you should go in?" she asks. "You look awful."

"No, no, I'm sure," he says. "I—"

He wants out of the house, away from me. I hear it all in his voice.

"I just need to get something," he says. "From my study. Stay here. Just a minute. I'll just be a minute."

I know he is coming to check to see if I am still here. If I am real. If last night really happened. What I don't know is what he is hoping for.

———

Alec is gone. The house is empty. I sit down at the piano to wait. I used to lie on the floor and watch my mother playing the piano and the sound of the notes—the way they'd vibrate through my body—got all mixed up with the expression on her face. When she played, really played, no one existed apart from her. She was perfectly alone and perfectly happy.

I thought that this exalted state of being was something that would come to me with growing up. And now I realize that it never did.

The piano is here because the thing Alec wanted most of all was for me to be happy.

But why am *I* here?

I'm sitting on the stairs, waiting, when Alec comes home from work. He opens the door and sees me, and I suddenly understand what the word *blanch* means. He blanches.

He herds me into his study. Closes the door behind him. Looks at me and I look at him.

"I mean, this can't be happening," he says. "It must be a dream. This is everything I wished for." He glances quickly at the closed door. "But how? Why? And what's it got to do with Dee?"

"Dee? I don't want to talk about Dee. I want to talk about us."

"Fay, why was Dee talking about ghosts? Did she know about you coming back? You haven't done anything to frighten that child, have you?"

"Are you kidding? It's the reverse, if anything."

"So she can see you?"

"I think I'm her new best friend."

I should tell him. I should tell him about the cutting. I should tell him she is a sad little girl in need of a family. That she thinks she's lost hers, that she herself is a little lost. I think about all the things I should say. But instead I say, "So you married her. Janet."

"Yes," he says, unable to look at me as he speaks. "I married her. This summer. Just a small ceremony. We didn't even have cake."

Cake. As if I give a damn about the cake.

"You'll have to tell her," I say.

"Tell her what?" he asks.

"Tell her to go," I say. "You'll have to tell Janet to go."

"We're married."

"No," I say. "*We* are married."

"Fay," he says. "Let's not rush things."

When you come back from the dead rather unexpectedly, there are certain things you may not want to hear. *Let's not rush things* is right at the top of the list.

"How long did you wait?" I ask.

Alec sighs. "How long did I wait?"

"Before you moved on."

He sighs again. Pulls at his hair so that it stands madly away from his head the way it did when we were young.

"Do you remember when we first met?" he asks.

"Don't change the subject," I say.

"I'm not," he says.

I lie down on his couch and cross my arms over my face.

"When we first met my whole relationship to time changed," he says. "I'd waited for things before. What is adolescence, after all, but a long train of waiting for things? But I'd never waited days for something, feeling every second in every minute of every hour as painfully and acutely as I had at the beginning of seeing you, of waiting to see you again."

"You've missed me," I say.

"No," he says. "I remember what missing you was like. Missing you was the fear of not seeing you again and the pleasure of imagining our reunion comingled into one. Sorrow sweetened by anticipation. I understood what it felt like to miss you. But what I felt when you died was something else again. That was something that I didn't have words for, much worse than anything I could ever have imagined. You have no idea."

And I realize that I don't. I can't imagine my house without me in it. I can't imagine Alec here alone.

"I don't think she's right for you," I say, changing tack.

"Fay." His voice is grudging. I am going too far.

"How can you be with someone who isn't me?" I ask.

"You're not even you anymore."

"Thanks very much."

He looks at me. Really looks at me. Shakes his head. "That's not what I mean. I want to believe you are real. You look so young. So beautiful."

"You look like hell," I say.

"I'm fifty. Fifty. Can you believe it?"

I will never be fifty now. I suppose there are worse fates than being thirty-seven forever. Twenty-nine was a particularly bad year. And if I had to be thirteen again I'd kill myself, even if I were already dead.

"You don't look fifty," I say. I realize I am lying as I say it. He does look fifty. Fifty-something even. "You just look like you," I say.

"I never expected to have to live without you," he says. "Being older than you should have given me a sort of insurance. I should have gone first." His voice breaks and becomes a wrenching sound like something has pulled loose inside of him.

"That was the worst—" he says. He stops, takes a ragged breath and starts again. "—the worst thing to ever happen to me. When you died I was sure I would die too."

I can see it on his face. The traces it left behind. All those new lines around his eyes, cross-hatched with suffering.

"I didn't mean to leave you," I say. "I didn't mean to die."

"People use language so lightly. But I really was. Lost. Without you. For a long time I just went on. Day after day after day. I wasn't really living. Just existing. Waiting to be with you again."

"In heaven?"

To my surprise Alec says softly, "I never said I didn't believe in heaven." This is an old argument. Perhaps one he expected to never have to revisit.

"You never said you did. I always believed we'd be together again one day."

"I wanted that too," he says.

"Wanting isn't believing," I say.

"I wanted to believe. But in my wildest dreams, I couldn't ever have imagined something like this. Life after death."

"And now?"

"Now?" he says. "Now you're here with me."

I want to take a fingertip and smooth out his new lines like a hot iron over silk. But I don't dare touch him, much as every bit of me longs to do just that. I pull myself over to sit beside him, leaving a safe distance between us. I think about how his neck used to smell.

Then he looks back at me and smiles that old smile.

"I am so happy to see you again," he says.

Maybe it's best to think of this quotidian time with Alec as a gift and just enjoy it. *Quotidian.* I never considered the beauty of that word before.

"Don't leave," I say. "Stay with me."

And for a spell, he does.

CHAPTER SEVEN

WE ARE IN the study. This could be the world to me, I am thinking when suddenly the door swings open. No knock.

Dee steps into the room and closes the door behind her.

"We can hear you," she says. Alec looks deeply uncomfortable to be in the room with the two of us. I realize that I am more real to him because someone else sees me.

"What?" Can Janet hear me now too?

"Not you, Fay," Dee says. "Just Alec. When Janet comes downstairs she will hear you in here talking to yourself." She looks at Alec, puts a finger over her lips, and nods solemnly. "And if she comes in and sees that guilty look on your face, I don't know what will happen."

"This is an unusual situation, Dee," Alec says.

"No kidding," says Dee.

"You have to know I would never betray your mother," says Alec.

Does she have to know that? Do I? Dee makes a who-cares shrug. I'm trying to work out what she does care about. Why did she come in here?

The door closes softly behind her.

"What was I thinking?" says Alec.

I put a finger over my lips, reminding him. Then I take a notepad from his desktop and write a question for him. "What was I wearing the first time you saw me?" I ask. I'm ready for a change of subject.

He looks at the paper. Writes: Dress. Blue. Flowers.

There is no way I was wearing a flowered dress. I look at the paper too. Think. I remember an old floral silk robe I wore for the few years we were together. It came from a thrift store and was so old that the silk was falling apart but it was also so soft and so beautiful.

"No," I say. "No, I was not wearing a flowered dress, you fool."

He smiles. Writes: Something on your head?

I had a fedora in those days. It was a man's fedora and I wore it constantly until the night I left it in a bar and never saw it again.

Alec's pencil moves across the page and I see he has sketched me there. Naked. A flowerpot on my head with an enormous daisy sprouting from it.

I have no idea what I was wearing. When I remember that day I see only him.

Alec looks at the picture and smiles. Then he takes back the pencil and rubs it rapidly back and forth until the page blackens. He looks up at me guiltily.

"It's okay," I say. "I'm still here."

I'm following Janet from room to room. She seems to be looking for something. Or maybe she's trying to get away from me. She never looks behind her, but once in a while she runs a hand over her nape as though something has made all the hairs stand up there.

I am making an inventory of missing items in my head. And then there's the fact that everything has changed colour, everything muted down to these stiflingly boring neutrals. Like a show home.

She straightens things, seemingly involuntarily, as she goes. Nudging the dining chairs into place with her hip, centring the basket for keys on the table in the foyer, picking up Alec's mail and shuffling it into a neat rectangle. I follow behind her and undo all that she does.

I look in through the French doors and see them sitting on opposite sofas in the living room. Man and wife. Janet has her arms crossed defensively in front of her chest. Alec looks like hell. Bleary-eyed and miserable. No sign of Dee.

"I wish you would tell me what's bothering you." This is Janet's voice. She sounds serious but not emotional, a tone I'd never managed to master. "I know you say you're fine, but you're not, really. It feels like you're somewhere else."

I lean forward, worried I will miss something.

Sensing that I am there, Alec looks up and shakes his head slightly—not so you'd notice, unless you were looking straight at him. But I can see that he is sending me a message. *Go away. You're not wanted here.*

I walk straight into the room and stand directly behind Janet.

Alec's jaw clenches and makes that clicking sound that signals anger. Janet looks up at him in surprise. He puts his face in his hands and I know he is trying to force himself to relax.

"I can't talk about it just now." He is struggling to look her in the eye.

I know he wants me to leave but I don't. Instead I move closer to Janet, so close that she would feel my breath on the back of her neck if breathing was something I still did. She shivers. Alec looks at me with something perilously close to despair. He really doesn't want me here.

Maybe I want her to know I am here. I am tired of this sad dance. It takes two to tango but three to do the butterfly. Whatever that means.

"Al," she leans forward, takes both his hands in hers. "What's the matter?"

"Nothing," he says, standing to embrace her. "Nothing is the matter, sweetheart."

Sweetheart. I know that is to punish me. And so, I go.

The house is dark and quiet when I return. I have to circle through the main floor before I find Alec sitting on the piano bench, his head cradled in his arms which are resting on the closed keyboard. It is all I can do not to rush toward him. *Let's not rush things.* I remember how easy it used to be. To be embraced and enclosed.

"So," I say.

He looks up at me. Hurt and pain in his eyes.

"I shouldn't have intruded that way," I say. "I was being childish."

Alec shakes his head.

"Why is this happening?" he says. "What did you come back for?"

I don't have an answer for that. Try to think what he might want to hear.

"To have just one more day with you? To say goodbye?"

"I loved living with you. But this, Fay? I had to say goodbye a long time ago. This is cruel. Some sort of cosmic joke. I feel as though I'm being punished. Is that what that is?"

Unable to answer him, I fade.

"Where does Janet go?" I ask Dee. We are down in the cellar. Dee is doing something on her phone.

"What do you mean where does she go?"

"Well, does she have a job? She goes somewhere all the time. Does she work?"

Dee looks at me blankly. This odd little girl. What does she really imagine is happening here?

"She has a gallery," she says. "That's where she goes. Mostly."

"A gallery? An art gallery?"

"Is there some other kind?" asks Dee.

Janet. She has the life I always wanted.

Dee puts down the phone and looks at me appraisingly. "Is that your real hair colour?" she asks. "Is it what they mean when they say auburn?" Clearly time to change the subject.

"I don't even remember what it was," I say. "Something mousy. I don't know." I've been dyeing it since high school. I can't imagine what it would look like if I'd left it alone.

"I thought I'd stop colouring it when I turned forty—or fifty, maybe. Aging with dignity and all that." Not something I need to worry about now.

I think of Alec saying to me, "When I look at you I just see you."

"Janet colours hers, too," says Dee, as if this is some fascinating thing that we have in common. "I think most older women do. It's weird, isn't it? Like you'll see someone from behind and think maybe she's your age, like young, and then she turns around and there's like all this loose wrinkly skin and that. I think it might be better to dye it grey when you're young, and then when you turned around people would be shocked at how young you look in comparison."

I suppose there is a logic in this. I feel a flush of shame at my own vanity, and a pang of sadness that I'll never see my hair turn grey the way my mother's did.

"Janet's not as old as you, though," says Dee.

"I'm only thirty-seven," I say. "Or I was. How old did you think I was?"

"Oh, I dunno," says Dee. She squints at me. "Forty-something? Fifty?"

Fifty. Thirty-seven always seemed old to me. On that downhill slide to forty. I cried on my last birthday. But then I always cried on birthdays. When I turned twelve, I cried so hard and then blew my nose in the twenty-dollar bill my father had given me and without thinking threw it in the wastebasket. Later, it took hours to find it again.

"Janet's thirty-two. She's younger than you," says Dee. And then, twisting her knife, she laughs, "And she's alive."

Morning. Alec and I are alone in the study. We are ensconced. I look around, trying to work out why I feel safe here.

"This room looks the same," I say. I force myself not to let my eyes stray to where the picture of the two of us should be.

Alec's eyes flick around the room as though he is seeing it for the first time.

"I didn't change anything anywhere in the house for the longest time," he says. "I wanted it all to stay the same. Only it wasn't the same. The taste of the air, the quality of the light, the weight of the atmosphere. Nothing was the same."

"So, it was—" I break off, reluctant to say her name aloud. As though it might conjure her up somehow.

"It was for my own good," he says, like he is answering a question I haven't asked. Then, as if realizing what I have been thinking. "No, it was me. I did it. I couldn't live with living without you day in and day out. Every time I opened the freezer and your pint of dark chocolate sorbet was sitting there waiting for you it would make me cry like it was the first day all over again."

I hadn't thought of this. Of him being left with everything and nothing all at once.

"It's good you got rid of things," I say. I don't mean it, but I think he needs to hear it.

"Oh, most of it is still here," he says. "Just not where I have to see it every day. I kept the important things. Packed it all up in boxes."

Not all the important things. I think about that old red velvet sofa. The times we'd lain end to end, each reading our own book. How the embossed pattern had been rubbed right off of each of the armrests when we inherited it from his Aunt Maud and how I liked to think of other heads resting where ours now lay.

I think about our bed and the nights we'd been together there, asleep and awake and alive.

I'm glad it's gone. The bed was ours, it can't be theirs.

I look at the closed study door and imagine that beyond it each room of our house is exactly as it was when I left. My things matter to me.

"I told you that I wished I was dead," he says. I turn to look at him. He's not looking at me, but over my left shoulder at a spot on the ceiling. "Well, it wasn't exactly an idle thought. I obsessed about it. For a year or so, I did my best to drink myself to death. After you . . . when I was . . ." He stops. I take a step to the left so that his eyes meet mine.

I find this hard to imagine. We used to enjoy having a drink together, but it was only ever me who had more than two. What's that old line: you take a drink and then the drink takes a drink and then the drink takes you. That was how Alec felt about drinking. So the idea of him bludgeoning himself insensible with alcohol is shocking to me.

He goes on. "That old involuntary reflex thing. Breathing. The way that you push yourself to the surface when all you want to do is stay on the ocean floor. The way the body keeps on keeping on even when you will it to stop. I thought I would die when you died. And yet here I am."

He sits up. Looks at me properly. Smiles a rueful smile. I always thought that was such an odd expression, but if ever a smile was full of rue it is this one.

We stay sequestered in the study until we hear Janet come down the stairs.

"Don't you have to go to work today?" I whisper.

"I'm staying with you. We'll have the day," he whispers back.

Noises reach us from the kitchen. Janet and Dee talking about something. The coffee maker. High heels going up and down the hallway. Pausing outside the door and then moving on.

"I'll go talk to her before she leaves for work. Don't go anywhere."

"What are you going to tell her?" I ask.

"What should I tell her?"

"The truth," I say. He doesn't laugh. None of this is funny. Still, I am so happy to have him to myself for the whole day that it hardly matters.

———

Alec comes back from talking to Janet and I deliberately do not ask how it went. Janet does not exist. I'm not thinking about Dee. This is an ordinary day. We have been living in this house together and nothing will interfere with that.

Alec calls the paper and tells them he won't be in. He tells them he has a sty in his eye.

"Why did you tell them that?" I ask.

"First thing that came into my head," he says. "It doesn't matter."

"You could have said you've had a visit from an old friend," I say.

"Old friend," he says, musingly. "Do you realize I've now known you for longer than you've known me? All those days and weeks and months since you've been gone and not a single day where I haven't thought of you. How do we count that? How do we count the anniversaries I celebrated alone?"

He puts his phone down on his desk and goes back over to lie down on the couch. I sit down in the desk chair and pivot back and forth on it. I am getting better at this sort of thing. If Janet happened to open the door right now she would see the chair moving on its own. I see this thought cross Alec's mind and he scowls so I stop.

"Do you remember the ladybugs?" I say.

When we bought the house, it had been painted yellow. A sickly sort of yellow that made the poor house look like it had come down with a bad case of jaundice. The day the realtor showed it to us the strangest thing happened. One whole side of the house was blanketed in ladybugs. It really flustered the realtor, but I thought it was kind of wonderful. It never happened again after we returned the house to its original glorious blue, so I guess it was something to do with the colour.

"In the verse, you mean? 'Fly away home'?"

"No," I say. But I realize he doesn't remember, and I don't elaborate. Maybe it happened, maybe it didn't. I can close my eyes and see it either way.

We are having our coffee at the kitchen table. Alec is having his coffee. I am watching. Everything is fine. I am just happy to be here. Alec hasn't gone upstairs to shave or get dressed. He says it doesn't matter. His beard stubble is almost white and it's like I can see his future self in his face.

We are silent together for a moment. When I was young I came across the phrase "a companionable silence" in a novel of my mother's. It had struck me as the saddest thing I'd ever heard. I had no idea.

"I used to dream," Alec says. He stops, takes a sip from his coffee, and I think of the way actors use props in films, deliberately drawing out those pauses for dramatic effect.

I wait. Will myself to say nothing.

"I used to dream that you hadn't really died. I'd walk into a room and there you'd be. Peeling an orange or reading the newspaper. Doing something so ordinary that it would take my breath away. Maybe they were memories. Memories of moments that were so unremarkable I hadn't bothered to register them, but there they were, stored away in my unconscious like I'd recorded them without realizing. One time we were washing the dishes."

"That sounds so boring," I say.

"It was." He smiles reminiscently.

"I'm here now," I say.

"Yes," he says. "You're here now. But for how long? And how will I bear it when you go again?"

Once I bought an old copy of *To the Lighthouse* at a second-hand store and when I opened it a newspaper clipping fell loose from between the pages. *Novelist Missing*, said the headline. It went on to describe the disappearance of Virginia Woolf.

Missing, I thought. Not dead. Not yet dead. Perhaps, I thought. Perhaps she may still be found alive.

Hope. That mad, unquenchable thing.

"What shall we do with our day?" asks Alec.

He opens the fridge and stares into it for a moment. When we were young we lived in an apartment so small that you could see the kitchen from the bed. I think of it now and realize that we had everything we needed there, and I just didn't know it.

Finally, he takes out the milk and puts it down on the counter. He fetches a box of muesli out of the pantry.

"Want anything?" he asks over his shoulder.

I don't answer.

"Oh," he says. "Of course not."

He reaches up to the cupboard and takes down a bowl and pours out the muesli and I feel a moment of intense pleasure at the familiar sound.

"Remember our first night together?" I ask.

"What a question. As if I am ever likely to forget."

He sits down across from me at the table with his breakfast. How many times did we sit together just like this? How many times did I waste these precious minutes

thinking ahead to some small task or some petty annoyance involving the day ahead?

"My favourite part was waking up with you. Waking
up with you sleeping beside me. And this strange feeling.
This sort of relief." He says this and then seems to hear
himself say it. His eyes fill with tears.

"Yeah, but the sex was good too," I say, and he laughs.

I felt it too. That I'd found the person I was going to
spend the rest of my life with. And I did.

We've moved into the conservatory and are bathing in the afternoon light. I can almost imagine the warmth of it on my skin. It's a perfect day.

"Tell me something," I say. "Tell me what's been happening with everybody we know since I've been gone."

And so, he does. He tells me about how Mira had kept coming around and wanting to talk to him after I died and how finally he'd had to tell her he couldn't stand the sight of her anymore. That he'd meant to say something polite to make her go away, to offer up some platitude, but instead he'd simply said: "I can't stand the sight of you," and then realized he'd said something irrevocable. "It was true. I shouldn't have said it, but it was true."

Poor Mira. I wonder who listens to her bang on about her life now that I am gone.

He tells me about his brother Jake and how he lost his teaching job because of something that had never come out. He'd done something. Nothing serious enough for a criminal charge. Something serious enough to get him fired. His wife had left him, and his teenage son wouldn't talk to him. He was working night shifts in a gas station over on the east side. I think of how smug Jake had always seemed, and how hard it is to imagine him with all that self-satisfaction knocked out of him.

He tells me about how his first editor—the one who hired him and brought us out here—has developed early-onset Alzheimer's, that it's now reached the point where he thinks Alec is someone different every time he visits. That our friends Bill and Billie divorced and then, after selling their house and getting rid of practically everything they owned, decided to get back together again and are now living on a houseboat down at Deep Cove.

He tells me about how my friend Carly developed Lou Gehrig's disease and how her ex-husband moved back into her house to look after her. I'd been wondering about Carly. I'd known her in high school and started running into her all the time when we moved back here. Suddenly she was nice to me and it was unsettling. She'd been one of the cool girls. The girls I envied and sort of despised. And then when we met as adults I realized what a lovely person she was. And how her life had only ever *seemed* perfect.

He tells me that the old woman who'd moved into the Vancouver Special I grew up in died, and how the next day one of her daughters pulled up with a moving truck and emptied the house before the other sister even knew her mother was dead. That the house was sold for an outlandish sum and was then knocked down. The house that went up in its place was twice its size and the colour of a bridesmaid's dress. Somebody owned it, presumably, but nobody lived there.

"Tell me something real," I say. "Something that matters."

He tells me about my mother. How she was so heart-broken in the beginning that she couldn't bear to be in the same room as Alec. How she blamed him without any real reason. Well, except that she needed someone to blame. "I understood it," he says. "I wanted someone to blame too," he says. They don't talk anymore, he tells me. It's too difficult.

Thinking about my mother hurts. My death one more sadness in her life. "Tell me something else," I say. "Quickly."

He tells me my sister has two little girls now. Joni they adopted from China four years ago, and then Fay was born last year. A surprise baby after all those years of trying. "Named after you," he says, as though I might not have guessed.

The whole time I was growing up I wished I was Vicki. My beautiful, brilliant sister. I grew up wearing her hand-me-downs. She was always taller, more developed, more mature. More everything. She was always that one step ahead. Got married before I did. Bought a house before I did. But I died first and left her behind. The only time I beat her.

"Stop," I said. "Stop now. Don't tell me any more." It hurts to hear about all these people, to still feel close, knowing they all think of me as gone.

———

I realize it's past the time when Janet and Dee should be home.

"They've gone out," he says, finally. Stating the obvious. "Janet took Dee out somewhere for dinner. Maybe a movie. No idea when they'll be back."

This time is a gift.

"She's unhappy because I won't tell her why I'm unhappy," he says. "This is impossible."

"Are you?"

"Am I what?"

"Unhappy?"

"Only when I'm not deliriously happy," he says. "You're back. You came back. The thing that is never supposed to happen happened."

"Amazing, right? This is my idea of perfect happiness," I say. "Now. This moment. And this one. And this one."

Alec begins to laugh.

"Life is wasted on the living," I say.

CHAPTER EIGHT

AS A FAVOUR to me, Alec is calling my mother.

He says that he hasn't seen her in a long time, even though she lives only twenty minutes away. I just need to see her once more. I hear him on the phone explaining that he has something he wants to give her. Something he thinks I would have wanted her to have. I've asked him to give her the photos he boxed up after I died. It was the first I'd mentioned knowing about them, and I saw a flicker of pain in his eyes as he remembered packing them away.

"I'm sorry," Alec says into the phone. There is some response I can't hear but then he catches my eye and nods.

"I know," he says. "No. Just me . . . Good. See you in an hour or so."

I didn't think she would come so soon. I don't know if I'm ready for this.

I watch as Alec takes the banker's boxes out of the study cupboard and stacks them neatly alongside his desk.

"Alec," I say. Louder than I meant to.

He turns to me, startled. "What?" he asks.

"Nothing. Nothing, really. Nerves, I suppose." For a moment I was suddenly afraid I might vanish again. I needed him to look at me so that I knew I was here.

When I was small, I had a fear of dying—of the earth opening up and swallowing me whole—but this stopped after my father died, and was replaced by a fear of my mother dying.

I used to go in and watch her when she was sleeping to make sure she was still breathing. One time she woke up and saw me standing there in my nightgown and screamed so loud she woke up Vicki. She made me promise not to do it ever again. But it took me years to trust that she would still be there in the morning. And when she left the house I would be uneasy until she returned. When I was away from her I imagined all sorts of terrible things happening to her. Once I saw a woman hit by a car and the noise that it made—the way the sound of the impact was both solid and liquid at the same time— stayed with me, and it seemed to me that my mother was impossibly vulnerable. Anything could happen to her.

I lie down on the psychiatrist's couch and listen with my eyes closed to the sound of Alec shifting the boxes. He is humming something, but so quietly that I can't make it out. He knows I am anxious and knows me well enough not to tell me not to worry.

The doorbell rings and I'm still not ready.

"Wait here," says Alec. "Do you want me to tell her? Prepare her? What should I say?"

"Don't say anything," I tell him. "Just bring her in here."

He goes out, and in a sudden fit of nerves I find myself hiding in the cupboard, leaving the door open just enough so that I can see into the room. I'm not ready to be seen by my mother, or worse still, be not seen. I think about the word *ajar* to stop myself from crying. Some joke from when I was a child about when is a door not a door.

And then the door opens again and there she is. She's older too. I'd forgotten that would happen. She's cut her hair short and is wearing glasses that make her face look completely different. Or maybe her face is completely different. Her expression is more closed than it used to be. Guarded. I could pass her on the street and not know her, I think to myself.

"Sit down," says Alec, gesturing. I see him looking around the room and then registering the opened closet door.

She ignores him and crosses the room and vanishes from my line of sight. Is she over by the window? I'm tempted to push the door forward so that I can see. But Alec throws a glance in my direction and I hold still. Then he disappears too.

"Please," says Alec. "Sit. I have something to show you." I see her again and Alec is gently cradling her elbow, guiding her in the direction he wants her to go.

She sits. She's lost some weight and is just generally smaller. I could pick her up and carry her from place to place.

Alec crosses over to the desk and I can't see him, although I hear a drawer opening. He crosses back with a large plastic bag in his hand. I recognize the yellow-and-black logo from the photo store up on West 10th.

"The family pictures that used to hang in the stairwell are all in these boxes. I can carry them out to the car for you. Maybe Vicki would like them? For the girls? These are just snapshots. I had copies made for you ages ago," Alec says to my mother. "Any of the pictures I could find with her in them. Some of them you probably have. I copied everything. To be safe." He's having trouble talking and he's not looking directly at her. This is costing him. My mother has tears in her eyes.

"I should have given these to you sooner. I should have called," he says. "I'm sorry. I . . ." He stops. Takes a breath and starts again. "I wish we'd taken more pictures.

I should have taken her picture every single day I knew her. I have them all up here," he says, tapping his temple. "But those are harder to share."

I see my mother breathe in and consider what to say.

"When my husband died, I thought I would die too," she tells Alec. "I didn't know how to be on my own. I didn't know how I would raise my girls all on my own. And I felt guilty."

Alec starts to say something but holds it back. He nods instead and waits.

My father died of an aneurysm. He went in his sleep and everybody always said he wouldn't have suffered. Wouldn't have known. And I used to think about that— about him dreaming and the dream suddenly turning into a door. I think about my mother waking that morning to find him both there and gone. The nightmare quality that morning must have had.

"I would have given anything to have him back. God knows he wasn't perfect. But he was mine."

"I know," says Alec. He looks over his shoulder toward the cupboard. To where I am hiding. For a moment I think he is going to tell her about me.

"Thank you," says my mother, "for these . . ." She lifts the bag and then lets it drop again. I know my mother. She won't open it until she is home and can look through them on her own. "And thank you too, for . . . She knew she was loved, didn't she?"

I am nodding my head like a fool in the dark cupboard.

Alec looks in my direction and he nods too. "Yes," he says. "She knew."

"That's important," says my mother. "That's what we want for our children. But I guess you're learning that for yourself now."

A gentle acknowledgement of his new family. I can see the surprise register on Alec's face.

Against all reason I step out into the room so that she can see me. Alec's head turns in my direction and I see panic in his eyes. My mother looks at him and then turns her head to see what he is looking at. I smile at her but as I do I realize that she sees nothing. She looks back toward Alec inquisitively. I step out and into nothingness.

When I return, Alec is lying on the psychiatrist's couch. At first I think he is asleep. Then, without moving his head to look in my direction, he speaks. "You all right?" he asks.

"I am," I say. "Thank you. Thank you for doing that."

We are silent for a spell. "I wish she could have seen you," Alec says finally.

"It was enough," I say.

Finally, he gets up and looks out the back window. I go to stand beside him. I look out at the sun playing on the leaves of the arbutus tree. "This is such a perfect yard," I say. A perfect yard for children, the realtor had told us.

Alec nods. I know he's remembering too.

"We should have named them," he says. We both look out into the yard. Everything looks tall to me. So lush and overgrown. So alive. "They died too."

"Yes," I say. It takes me a moment to realize he's talking about the pond full of koi fish.

"I loved those fish," I say. I turn back to the window.

"They were easy to love," he says. "They never spoke in anger. Always listened to my stories. Didn't come to bed with cold feet."

I laugh.

"You didn't come back because you needed to know you were loved, did you?" Alec asks. I turn to him. He is still looking out the window.

"If anything, it was because I knew I was loved."

"This is impossible, Fay. Untenable. I can't live in this house with two wives, like some Noël Coward character."

"So then you'll have to choose."

I leave him alone to think about that a little.

I should go. Cross over. Whatever it is that people are meant to do when they die. But I seem to lack the will. I try to find my way back to when Alec was mine and mine alone. If I can wander in the past, then why can't I just open a door and find myself where I want to be? Which is here. In my house with my husband, and alive.

Instead, I travel back to my grandmother's kitchen.

I am sitting at the table and trying to remind myself not to kick against the legs of the chair because she doesn't like it and she can hear it even when she is in the next room. I plant my feet flat on the floor and feel suddenly taller, older.

"Will I be tall like you someday?" I ask.

She comes into the room carrying a grapefruit in a white bowl. The grapefruit has been cut in half and she has taken a sharp knife and outlined all the segments. She had special spoons for this and only this.

"I think you will be taller," she says, laughing. "And you will live a long, long life and be happy most of the time."

"Why not all of the time?" I ask.

"Because then you would take it for granted," she says.

Then I am twenty. Twenty was good—I'd figured myself out and settled down to enjoy life. I stopped buying clothes I would never wear and wearing clothes I should never have bought. I picked a hair colour and stuck to it. I decided I was tired of living with roommates and got a very small apartment of my own. I was in my last year of my degree. I was looking at grad schools. I owned more books than furniture. My closet was bigger than my kitchen and I was up three flights of stairs but once I was up those stairs it was perfect. The living room had windows on three sides, and they all looked out into trees. Not onto trees but into them, because they were right there on the other side of the glass. I didn't even need to hang curtains. I was pretty happy at twenty. I close my eyes and think about the light coming in through those trees.

I am lying on my back on the floor of my apartment. I can see several paperback books that have fallen under the sofa and have been there long enough that they are lightly furred in dust. I wonder idly what they are, but don't care enough to reach out my hand to find out.

I'm slightly hungover and it's strange but I like being hungover more than I like being drunk. I like the feeling, the loss of control, that has left me on my living room floor on this sunny Sunday afternoon when I am supposed to be somewhere else. I'm supposed to be meeting a boy. He *is* a boy, too, not a man at all.

The way the sun is illuminating the dust motes in the air makes me think of how I used to imagine God when I was a child. I never understood all those pictures of bearded old men or anything else because for me he was clearly that stream of light that you would sometimes see leaking through the clouds. There was no reason for him to ever be any more visible than that, it seemed to me.

I pull my hair forward so I can see the ends. The light shines through so that each strand sort of glows and even the split ends are beautiful, like some strange insect universe seen through a microscope. My mouth is dry, and I think of getting up to get something to drink. I picture myself standing up and walking to the kitchen and opening the fridge. There is orange juice in there, and a jug of filtered water that will be beautifully cold and clear. I can't think of anything better. But I remain where I am. I have this funny feeling that I am suspended in this moment in the same way that the specks of dust are suspended in the air. If I move, everything may suddenly change. I look out the window at the green world there and can't imagine being anywhere but here.

I seem to have fallen asleep on the carpet. I can feel the bristles of the woollen nap digging into my cheek and know I will have a mark there that will take all day to fade. I will go to class looking like someone who has been struck or had an accident. I will look like someone that something has happened to. Go to class? Do I have to go to class today? For a moment I have a strong feeling of déjà vu, but I shake it off. I need to have a shower and clear my head if I am going to finish writing the essay I was meant to be writing last night. The essay about . . . the one on the sources of . . . It's so strange. I can't remember at all.

I pick up the dishes I left sitting on the table last night and carry them out to the sink. My mother would be scandalized that I went to bed without doing my dishes. Of course, there are many things I do that would scandalize her. At least some of them I do because they would scandalize her.

I think about the boy I stood up. I'd never intended to go. He was sweet and funny, but you could look at him now and realize that in twenty years he would still be exactly the same. Playing his guitar in little cafés. Working some joe job to pay the rent. Always making romantic little picnics to be eaten in bed or on a beach somewhere because he never had the price of a restaurant meal. Not the kind of boy it made any sense at all to fall in love with. Not with his golden curls or his warm laugh or the way he looked at you, or any of it.

I am tiring of living in the present tense. I am thinking about the future—about making plans and meeting someone and making a life. I am thinking of a house as a home and trying to picture myself there. I wake up in my narrow little bed and immediately feel something is wrong. Am I late? Was I supposed to be somewhere?

I sit up and look around. There are clothes strewn around the room and stacks of books tottering on every flat surface. I am wearing a t-shirt that has the name of my high school on it. I had to buy it for gym class but now for some reason, I have started liking it in equal proportion to how much I hated it then. I try to work out what this says about me. Is this nostalgia? Surely I'm too young. I'm only—

A voice in my head tells me that this is not real. This is not my life. I've been here for days and days now. I've had meals and watched movies and talked on the phone for hours and hours. I used to do that. I know that I am not really twenty. That I don't belong here. But it is tempting to stay. To just start again. To be twenty and then twenty-one and then twenty-two and so on. Then to meet Alec again for the first time. To be young. To be alive. I died. I don't belong here. This is not real.

Yesterday's half-consumed cup of morning coffee is still on the bedside table. I experimentally sip at it. I can swallow. I can taste. Somehow I am back in this body. Alive. The coffee is cold and bitter and possibly more delicious than I could ever imagine. For the past number of days, I have been living and simply taking everything for granted. I truly am young again. Now I want it all. I want to eat and bathe and have torrid, sweaty sex. I want to eat a fig. I'm overcome with a sick feeling of longing mixed with self-pity. I feel my skin begin to prickle like at the beginning of a fever. I lie down and close my eyes and let the tears run down into my ears. I luxuriate in feeling sorry for myself.

Oh lord, that was frightening. I look around to be sure I am here. That I am me. Me now. Dead me instead of past me. That was like being caught in some very comfortable web. I could have stayed forever. Could I have stayed forever?

I tell myself to stay in the present but instead I give in to the temptation to relive nights out with friends and nights in with Alec. I visit days from early in our relationship all muddled in with days from when we knew each other better than any other person on the planet. There are days I visit more than once. I return again and again to a night we slept on quilts laid on the conservatory floor, listening to the rain against the glass. I go dancing with him in late-night Montreal clubs and walk home with him in Montreal dawns.

I go back and spend time with everyone I've ever loved: my parents, my sister, Gran. I seem to be able to go anywhere—revisit any moment from the life I lived. I go canoeing with my father. I listen to him read to me from *A Midsummer Night's Dream*. I go picking blackberries with my mother. A long, slow afternoon where we barely speak to each other and yet are never more than an arm's length apart. I seem to be able to stay for longer and longer inside a memory, but I am sluggish when I return.

I can go anywhere that I have already been. I can have that time back again. But then, after spending a languid afternoon sometime at the end of the twentieth century drinking whisky macs in a posh hotel room with Alec, I try to walk through a wall and instead of reappearing in the cellar as I expect to, I suddenly am nowhere.

It is cold and dark wherever this is, and I have to resist the temptation to scream because it would frighten me even more to hear my voice in this non-place.

I put my hands out in front of me and try to move forward to see if there is a wall or door or anything at all, but there is just the feeling of dark as absence and I have to pull my hands up to my face quickly to be certain they are still there.

I close my eyes and wish I were dead.

Then I open them again and I am in the study and the light from the window dappling the gleaming oak surface of Alec's desk is almost enough to make me weep because it is so real.

I tell myself that I shouldn't go memory surfing again. That it is dangerous. That I could end up in the dark woods. But like a wilful teenager, I refuse to listen. I want to be back to when we were together. When we are happy. I go back to the old days once more because despite the danger, I can't stop myself from revisiting the wonderful time when Alec and I were new.

The windows are all open and the apartment is sweltering. I can hear the children from next door playing in the yard. A ball thumps repeatedly against a wall and I feel like my heart is slowing down to match the regular sound of rubber thwacking against brick.

There is no sign of Alec. I'm lying in our bed wearing one of his undershirts and a pair of his boxers. Anything more than that sticks to my skin and makes me feel like screaming. Vancouver is never hot like this. I'm sorry I ever left.

Last night was bad. I got mad at Alec for talking to a woman at the party and stormed off. I thought he'd follow me and he didn't and now it's morning and he's still not here.

I think it was her height and her red hair and the shape of her hands that unnerved me. I shouldn't have told him she looked like a witch. It was certainly true, and the sort of thing Alec would have laughed at if we'd been getting along—but we weren't getting along, and he said I was being immature. And he was right.

Is he going to leave me? Is he going to run away with the witch who can talk about all those great Russian novels when I can't even say Dostoevsky out loud for fear of getting it wrong?

This tiny room is making me feel crazy. Alec says to think of it like an Elizabethan box bed. Box room, box bed, boxed in. It's fine when we are in here together. I do like this apartment. The stained-glass windows in the living room are the nicest bit. I always think that if you were outside looking in then it would seem perfect. Where is he?

He's never stayed away all night before. What if he never comes back? What if something has happened to him?

And then I am back. Here. Now. I can feel all the agony of that day but I'd forgotten all about it years ago. It was nothing. Alec came home. We made up. But thinking about how bereft I felt in that moment leaves me almost grateful to be the one who has died. I don't want to go back there.

I remain hidden. Watch the three of them playing family. He is sad and broken and she doesn't know why, but she knows that he needs her care. When they sit together in the evenings she puts her hand on the back of his neck and I imagine how it must feel. The coolness of her skin. The steadying feel of that constant gentle pressure. Her loving touch.

I shouldn't have ever had to see him with someone else, but I have.

For now, I stay in the shadows. No one sees me. No one knows I am here.

One evening I see him take her hand in his and press his lips into the centre of her palm. She moans and then laughs.

When they go up the stairs I don't follow, and I don't allow my mind to follow, either.

CHAPTER NINE

I AM WAITING for Alec in the study and when he opens the door, before he can see me or not see me, I speak.

"Hello, my life," I say.

I see him draw back in shock and then gather himself. "Where have you been?" he asks. I am looking into his eyes. Trying to gauge if he is happy to see me.

"I've been spending time in the past," I say without knowing I'm going to. I sit down beside him.

"Remembering things, you mean?"

"No, not remembering exactly. It's more intense. Like I'm really there."

He looks at me. Smiles. Frowns. "Time travel?" he asks.

"Kind of. I'm not sure it's good," I say, carefully. "I mean it is good. It's great. But also, every time I go into the past it's like less of me comes back."

"Can you choose where you go?"

"Not completely. Sometimes. Maybe. Where would you go?"

"Oh . . ." he says. He stares at his hands. "I don't think I would want to go anywhere. Not unless I could stay."

This surprises me.

"Not our first night in the house?" I ask. "Or the day we met? I can tell you what everyone else in the room was wearing. I can tell you what it said on the beer mat. What the specials of the day written on the chalkboard were. I can tell you what song was playing. I can see everything. Like it's still right there. Like we are still right there."

He stands, turns away from me, goes over and looks out the window. "I don't care about any of that. I know we were there. It happened. It was a long time ago."

"But I feel it. I feel everything. I'm there. I'm right there."

"I don't think you should do it anymore," he says. "What if you go into the past and can't get back?"

"Then I would be back there, living our lives all over again. At least I would be with you." I go to stand beside him.

He shudders.

"I won't do it again," I say quickly. "I won't go back anymore. I promise. I just want to be here with you."

I look at him and then he looks at me and it is exactly the same thrill as the first time he looked at me.

I am thinking that if Janet and Dee were to leave for good, Alec and I could go back to living here on our own. And it might get easier. This is what is in my mind as I take the little Chanel spritzer out from my old satchel hidden under Dee's bed. The perfume had been a birthday gift from my mother. It was what I remembered her wearing on special occasions when I was small, and I liked the idea of wearing it myself when I put on something nice and wore my hair up in a twist. Only I actually hardly ever used it because it made me sneeze.

I steel myself to go into the bedroom. I open what was my closet and am rewarded with the sight of all of Janet's black garments hung neatly in a row.

There isn't a lot of scent left in the bottle, but I think there's enough to send a message. Janet needs to know this is still my house.

THE GHOST IN THE HOUSE

I'm in the kitchen looking out the window and thinking about children playing in that yard. Climbing the tree. I can almost hear their shouts and laughter. Without even looking down at my hand I reach out to the window ledge and feel the circle of hard metal beneath my fingers. It takes just the tiniest of movements and I hear it hit the stainless-steel sink and then tinkle its way down the drain. Janet was a fool to leave her wedding band sitting there.

Alec is alone in his study when I find him. He doesn't look at me.

I sit down in his desk chair and try to think of something to say. I can't stand for him to be unhappy with me. "Today when I was the only person in the house I started hearing something upstairs," I say. "Something like the sound a rocking chair makes as it goes back and forth on a wooden floor. What do you call those things on the bottom? Rails?"

He is lying stretched out on the couch with his arm thrown across his eyes, so it is impossible to read his expression. He is wearing a beautiful green sweater and I'd like to remark on it, but it hardly seems the time. I would like to lie down next to him and throw my leg over him and rest there awhile with my head on his chest and his heart singing its old sweet song in my ear.

"I think you call them rockers," says Alec. His voice is small and tight.

"Okay, rockers," I say. "I could hear this sound. And I thought, what if it's a ghost? Which is stupid—for a dead person to be afraid of ghosts. But I never believed in them before, and now I do. And I can't imagine who else might be haunting this house and wasn't sure I was up to meeting them. I mean, people must have died in this house over the years. It's what . . . a century old, right?"

He still isn't looking at me.

"I was scared," I say.

"Scared? Like you want Janet to be? The way all your stupid little stunts are meant to frighten Janet half out of her wits in her own home?"

Her home.

He looks at me and I wish to be anywhere but here.

"But my things, my house, my—"

"Things! Things! It's a house, Fay. A thing. There are lives involved here, Fay. Real, human lives."

I find myself drifting from room to room. I go to the kitchen but find I am getting the urge to break things again, so drift on. In the living room I stop short. It's dark but there is enough moonlight for me to see that my dollhouse has been placed back in its old spot. It's turned the wrong way around, but it is there. Is this a message? And who for? I once told Alec—half joking—that rather than buying an urn he could put my ashes inside the dollhouse and then bury that. I suppose he ignored me, because the house is still here.

I sit on the piano bench to wait. I lightly finger the keys so they make sounds that you might hear but would also doubt you were hearing. I wait. I watch the light change outside the window as dawn finally arrives. I think about the first night I found myself here on the piano. About how little I knew then.

Finally, Janet comes down the stairs. She is dressed in one of her chic black outfits and her hair is perfectly smooth, but her face looks as though she's had a bad night. There is a moment's pause as she walks into the room and I see her register the dollhouse. She walks over and rests a hand on the roof as though to persuade herself it is real.

She doesn't scream or faint or do any of the things I might have hoped when she sees my dollhouse back in its old spot. She stands and looks at it for a moment. Turns away and then turns back as though she might possibly have dreamt it. Then she walks out of the room. I hear her on the stairs and then the sound of the bedroom door clicking shut.

"Of course it was her. Who else would it be?" Janet gets up from the breakfast table to fetch the coffee pot. I see Alec look helplessly out the window. How can he answer that question?

"I hate that she's unhappy," he says.

"She's unsettled. She's acting out. It will pass," Janet says. She fills his cup and drops a kiss on the top of his head before sitting down.

Alec nods. He stares out the window again and I realize that my dollhouse is out there. It must be out in the back lane by the bins. My house has been discarded.

"She and I have been through a lot. She's a tough little cookie."

"Like her mother," says Alec.

"Like her mother," Janet agrees and laughs.

"I wish she gave you more credit."

"She wants to believe her father is a good person. You can't blame her for that."

Alec shakes his head. "We're her family now. You and me. We'll get her through whatever she's going through. If she needs help then we'll get help."

He reaches out and takes her hand. He is so focused on Janet, on their conversation, that he doesn't look behind him. He doesn't even know I am here.

———

I find Dee in the cellar. She has her phone on a little tripod and is taking pictures of herself. She is wearing a pink top that looks like it was made out of recycled bath mat. She is smiling. She seems like she's a different person and this is the other thing I'd forgotten about being thirteen. You change like the weather.

"Was that you? The dollhouse?"

"That's for me to know," she says. Then she directs the phone camera at me and snaps a series of pics. Looks critically at the phone, flipping through them.

"Nothing to see here," she says, showing me the photo of the empty space where I should be.

"Was it you?" I ask.

"I don't know what you mean," she laughs. "Anyway, it worked. I think maybe we're going to see Dad. To give him another chance." She gives me a curious look. "So that's it," she says. "You can go now. Or stay. Your choice."

I stay away as long as I can bear, hoping that Alec's annoyance with me will dissipate in my absence. When I return, I find him sitting alone in his study with a glass of wine in his hand. He is wearing a tattered old sweatshirt of mine with the Ficciones logo on the front. I'd forgotten that shirt existed. The bookstore itself is long gone.

I sit down beside him and wait for him to say something. He doesn't, so we sit in silence for a long time. He finishes his glass and then refills it. There is a sort of electricity emanating from him. If he were a cat his hair would all be standing on end. Picturing this makes me laugh and he looks up at me, shocked.

"Are you still unhappy with me?" I say finally.

He sighs. "I would be," he says. "If I thought it would do any good."

I'm looking at him. Trying to gauge his mental state. The bleariness around the eyes is superficial but there is something deeper there too. He looks grief-stricken. I realize I am getting a glimpse of how he must have looked in the days after I died. When he was here in the house alone.

"They've gone away," he says. "To the island. Janet's sister still lives there. Janet thought it would help Dee to see family."

I've gotten what I wanted all along. I have Alec all to myself. So why do I feel so awful?

"I'm sorry," I say. "I'm so sorry for everything. All of it. And I'm sorry I came back."

"Don't say that," he says.

"I wanted to be with you," I say. I know I sound foolish. I am foolish. "I would have married you that first day if you'd asked me. I wish I had. I wish when people asked about the day we'd met we could have said that we went straight downtown and got married. Then they would have known what we always knew," I say.

He shakes his head at me.

"I wish I'd had your children. I wish we'd had a family. I wish I'd had more courage," I say.

Alec sighs again. "Why are you doing this, Fay?"

I look at Alec sitting there and think how alone he looks. I have done this to him.

I think about telling him again that it wasn't me who moved the dollhouse and then realize it doesn't matter.

"Alec—" I say. And then stop, because what can I say? How can I make this right?

"I wish we could go for a walk," Alec says, finally. He turns and looks at me. He is so close. "That's what I used to imagine after you . . ."

"Died?" I say.

"After you died, yes. I used to go out alone. I'd walk the paths in Pacific Spirit Park that we used to walk back when we first moved into this house. If there were no one around I would talk to you. I would pretend you were walking with me . . . maybe a few steps behind, so that if I stopped and turned my head I would see you."

Our walks were the time that we talked best—talked widely and freely about all the things that mattered and lots of things that mattered not at all. Sometimes we talked about the children we were going to have. We talked about ourselves as children and pretended to be hearing stories for the first time. I could picture Alec easily as a child. His serious little face. His narrow shoulders pulled up square. We talked about how my job working for Mira was not what I wanted to be doing and how miserable it made me even though I still couldn't manage to quit. We talked about whether I should go back to school and do something else. I told him all my big ideas for art projects. We talked about the first time we met. We talked about being cremated versus being buried. We talked about the word *cremains* and how horrible it was. We agreed that whoever went first would save the ashes of the other.

I want to ask now if he had me cremated. It makes me queasy to think about.

"I miss those ferns," I say instead. "Those huge, lush ferns that grow in the woods. Such strange, prehistoric-looking things."

"Yes," he says.

"And the sweet taste of the air when you get into the forest proper. The way the city just vanishes, and time becomes meaningless."

I see the two of us paused on a path, looking up to see where the treetops touch the sky. The rush of that feeling, how small you feel in comparison. I'm picturing the way that two trees can grow together to the point where you can't tell where one ends and the other begins.

"I miss you," says Alec. Present tense.

Where am I? I wonder. Where have I gone?

CHAPTER TEN

WE ARE ALONE. The two of us. Alec is changing the sheets in the bedroom so that we can sleep there tonight. Or so that he can sleep, and I can watch him.

The house feels different without Dee and Janet. It still looks wrong, but it somehow feels right.

"I was happy. I didn't even know how happy I was."

"You weren't happy all the time," he says, and he gets up and crosses over to the light switch. Then he takes off his pants and shirt in the dark before lying down on the bed in his boxers. My eyes are adjusting to the dim light in the room and he is just a moving shape. I wish he'd done it the other way around and undressed before turning out the light. He's embarrassed around me now. Given that in the old days he would cook breakfast buck-naked, this strikes me as profoundly sad.

"What do you mean?" I ask.

"You were always at least a little unhappy. You always wanted something you didn't have or imagined you didn't have. You complained all the time, Fay. All the time. You always thought that you were missing out on something. I thought this house would make you happy. I moved back here to make you happy—never would have come here of my own volition—and what good did it do?"

"I loved this house," I say. "I was happy here. I was so."

"Okay," says Alec. "You were happy."

"We were happy," I correct him.

"Are you coming to bed then?" he asks and I feel suddenly nervous.

"In a minute," I say.

I go into the bathroom to look around. I loved this bathroom. Then I open the medicine cabinet door and all the wrong things are in there. Lipstick. I take the cap off to look. There is a dent in the centre where her lip must fit. I put it back, resisting the childish urge to wind it up and smush the lid down on it. A bottle of sleeping pills. Alec's name on the label. Perhaps they're from when I died? But no, they're new. Now that is sad. There is a package of birth control pills. None of them have been taken.

I close the medicine cabinet and then I lie down in the tub with all my clothes on. It's dark out. I can see the stars out the skylight, and it takes no time at all to slip back into a memory of a bath. The water is steaming hot and smells of rosemary bath oil. I luxuriate in it, lying in the tub until the tingle of excitement is almost physical, and then I climb out and pad down the hall to the bedroom. In my mind I am naked. I can see the wet trail of footprints I leave behind me.

When I get to our bedroom, Alec is lying in bed. Just the two of us together. There is so little light that the room could be as it used to be, as I want it to be. I lie down on my side of the bed, careful not to stray too close to Alec. There is nothing I want more in the world than to stray.

"Remember," I say. "Remember how big and empty this house felt?"

"It was full of rooms you'd yet to ravish me in," Alec says, laughing.

I imagine us in each of the rooms of the house. Together. I want those days back. Those early days where we were hungry for each other all the time.

"I didn't know if I should tell you this, but I did try to contact you," Alec says. "I played Houdini's wife."

"What?"

"Houdini's wife. She tried to contact him after he died. One year she thought the medium had been successful. But then she changed her mind."

"When was this? You, I mean. When did you try to contact me?"

"A while ago."

A while. What exactly is a while?

"What happened?"

"I lost my nerve. The psychic asked me what I wanted to know. I had so many questions. I suddenly couldn't face it. I paid and beat it the hell out of there. I felt like an idiot," he says. "You know, Houdini spent all that time exposing fraudulent spiritualists. But really, I think he wanted to believe. I think we all do."

"Maybe we all only think we do. Because we don't know what it will be like."

Eventually Alec falls asleep. I listen to his breathing as it gets slower and more regular. I am tempted to go back in time to a night when we were truly together. But I'm right where I wanted to be—alone in the house with Alec.

I watch Alec sleep and wonder why I didn't do that more often when I was alive. All that time wasted. He looks sweet and unguarded. He looks like a boy. Innocent. Untroubled. Unburdened. I long to push the hair back from his forehead, to feel the smooth curls run through my fingers. This longing aches like a deep hunger. And there are deeper hungers below it. I want him, want to be with him. I never thought that much about my own body, but I desperately miss it now. I try to remember what it felt like when he touched my skin. How his touch was different than anyone else's. Every thought, every memory is immediately translated into mere words. The idea of touch is like something that was once described to me. Something I can only try to imagine.

Slowly, slowly it passes from being very late to being very early. I am in agony. I think about people willingly putting themselves into sensory deprivation tanks in order to relax. They have no idea how deprived you can feel when sensation is forcibly taken away from you.

Alec goes on sleeping peacefully while I go to pieces less than a foot away from him. I am tempted to call out his name, but the fear that I will be unable to make a sound stops me. The night drags grimly on. I find myself tempted to slip into the past, into some moment of intimacy, but am afraid of missing anything here. What if Alec wakes and I am gone?

"World enough and time," I say. "What's that from? Or is it time enough? Time enough and world . . . No, that can't be right. Sounds like Shakespeare. Do you think it is Shakespeare?"

Alec opens his eyes.

"Were you sleeping?" I ask.

"No, no," he says. Then: "Yes."

"Marvell," I say. "I think it's Marvell."

"Did you want to get up now?" he asks. "I mean, it's early, but if you want to get up I will get up." He blinks hard. He looks at me, but his eyes are as unfocused as those of a newborn.

"You've been asleep so long," I say. "Did you remember? Did you remember I was here?"

He nods. A little noncommittally for my liking. "Okay," Alec says. "I'm awake. I can hear your mind working over there." He throws back the covers and rapidly stands. He is a dark shape against the brightly lit window, a familiar silhouette.

He looks at me looking at him. "What are you thinking?" he asks.

"I'm thinking about pancakes," I lie.

"I didn't think you liked pancakes," he says.

"Yeah, but maybe I didn't give them enough of a chance. Now I'll never know."

"Ha," he says.

"Back in a minute," he says and goes straight in to shave. He always used to do that right after waking because I would complain about how bristly his morning beard was, but I don't bother reminding him that he's now unlikely to subject me to whisker burn.

While he is gone, I look around the room now that it is almost light enough to see. I'd painted all the walls each in a different shade of blue and it has now all been painted over in a very ordinary white. There is a huge painting over the bed, and it is also white. You have to look very closely to see that it's a painting at all. White on white. It doesn't make any sense to me.

Alec comes out of the bathroom with a towel wrapped around his waist. His face is flushed and smooth. All his chest hair is damp and tendril-y. I suddenly wonder if he went to shave for me out of habit, or if this is something he now does for her.

Even when she is not here, she is here.

Alec and I are sitting in the conservatory and I am happy thinking that we don't need to speak because we know each other so well that we can share a single thought when he suddenly says, "I have to call her, you know. I can't not call her."

I react before I can even think about what I am saying. "Has it occurred to you that she might be with her ex?" I ask. "What's he called? Have you met him?"

I look around at all the lush, growing things and think about Dee. That little face of hers in the old photo of the three of them as a family.

"She doesn't see him," he says.

"How do you know?"

"I know," he says. "She doesn't see him because he's a monster."

"What do you mean?"

"I don't want to talk about it."

He gets up and walks away from me. Just walks away. I wait for a moment, shocked, and then follow.

"What do you mean a monster?" I ask, catching up to him in the foyer. I position myself in front of him so he has to stop and look at me.

"There's the type of man who hits women," says Alec, not meeting my eye. "And then there's the type of man who does it in front of his own child."

I have nothing to say and so I say nothing. It comes to me clearly how much they need Alec. How selfish I've been. I could only see Alec as my husband. I couldn't see that anyone else might need him. Might even need him more than me. Dee could be in danger. They need to come home. Nothing matters more than this.

"Alec," I say, but he stubbornly refuses to turn. Refuses to look at me. I need to make him understand. "Alec," I say again, and I reach out and grab him by the shoulder. I see the shock pass between us like a current. I feel it, physically feel it as though it is my body receiving the jolt of energy.

Alec looks at me and his face freezes into a sort of a tragedy mask, misshapen and downturned. His eyes roll back so that just the whites are showing, and his face goes grey and slack. His hands spasm and shake like there is an electrical current running through his body. Then he is lying on the floor motionless.

I scream. I don't know what to do. I'm afraid to touch him. Afraid to make things worse.

And then I can feel myself fading out even as I desperately try to stay. He's lying there and I can't reach him. And then the darkness closes between us.

I am somehow neither here nor there. I feel strange. Drunk, almost. I start to slip into the past. Into the luxury of being with Alec again. I want our first night in this house again. I want that back. But then I stop myself because there is something of the opiate about these memory excursions of mine. They seem to dim whatever is left of me. I don't want to go back to that horrible dark again. I want to find Alec. If he's dead he should be with me. If he's alive then he must still be somewhere waiting for me to find my way back.

I am alone. I had this idea that if Alec died it might be a good thing. It might mean that we could be together again, in whatever form. But there is no sign of him, and I am now more alone than ever. The house is empty. This is an eerie feeling. Like it's been abandoned. Like the people who lived here have gone away and may never come back. I keep searching for him anyway. Is he in the hospital? Have I killed him? And if so, then why isn't he here with me?

Alec is alive. I hear him talking to someone. Janet? They must be back. They came back. Fine. I only care that Alec is alive. I go up the cellar stairs and toward his voice.

I can't believe how happy I am, like I've had an infusion of joy. Alec is alive. I thought I'd killed him and I haven't. When I reach the top of the stairs I stop to think. Janet. What am I going to do about Janet? And Dee. I will get to see Dee again. I'd thought I was going to be alone forever.

I open the door and the voices get louder. "You look terrible," says Janet. "Were you languishing without me?" She laughs and after the briefest of pauses he laughs with her.

He is sitting on the sofa and she lowers herself into his lap. Puts her arm around his neck. Kisses him. The whole time he is watching me. He has seen me come into the room. He must have wondered if I was still here and now he knows. I shake my head. I see by his face that he thinks I want him to push Janet away but that's not what I mean. I need to be alone with him to tell him what I mean.

I smile at him. I smile at both of them. And then I leave them alone.

I am in Dee's room. Wondering if she will come back here. I wish I'd tried harder to be of use to her. To see more clearly what she needed. I leave *Frankenstein* on her nightstand. I took it from Alec's study, so perhaps she will think it came from him. That doesn't really matter. What matters is that Mary Shelley will help her more through her dark days than any twee tween nonsense about the sexy undead.

Does the fact that Mary Shelley was nineteen when she wrote *Frankenstein* make her a young-adult author? I open the book and read: "Life and death appeared to me ideal bounds, which I should first break through, and pour a torrent of light into our dark world."

A torrent of light. I have broken the natural laws by my return. And there are, as always, consequences.

I stay in the dark for a long time. Hours or days or years. I am here and not here. I expect to be overtaken by fear, but it doesn't come. I realize that fear is nothing but anticipation and I have nothing left to anticipate. I am just here-not here. When I was young, I used to wonder where my shadow went when the sunshine blazed it free of my body. I feel like that now. I am my own shadow.

I can't garner the energy fully to be—it is like I am nothing but a scattering of particles. In one way this is frustrating. In another way it doesn't matter at all.

Sometimes I hear voices in the house, but they are too remote for me to make out who is speaking or what they are saying.

Time passes and the dark advances and recedes.

Dee is down in her lair, giving herself a complicated manicure involving little torn pieces of newspaper that she glues down to each nail and then varnishes over with clear polish. It looks ridiculous and scruffy and she is inordinately pleased with herself.

"That's looking great," I say. She looks up at me and blows her bangs out of her eyes. Her hair is so fine and pale that it's like dandelion fluff.

"How was the island?" I ask.

"Oh, fine. I saw my cousins."

"And your dad?"

"He was pretty busy. He couldn't make the time." She says this blithely, but I can hear the raw edge of pain beneath the words.

"Do you get along with anybody?" I ask, looking for a change of subject. Then I realize that sounds harsh. "I mean . . . is there anyone you pal around with?"

Now I sound inane. "Hang out with?" I try.

Dee gives me a withering look.

"I just mean you never seem to have anyone over here."

"I like to keep myself to myself," she says.

I wonder what that even means.

"This cutting thing," I say. "You said you were a cutter . . ."

"Oh that," she says.

"What do you mean, 'oh that'? Are you a cutter or not?"

"Not," she says.

"You're not?"

"Well, don't sound so disappointed." She snorts. Holds a hand in front of my face for me to look at her nails. I nod with what I hope passes for an air of approval.

"It's good," I say. "It's good you're not a cutter."

"You do know that word sounds stupider every time you say it, right?"

"So, you're okay, then? There's nothing you need to talk about?"

"I have a mother, you know," says Dee. "I hear enough of this from her. She's finding me someone to talk to, so enough already."

Why did I think Janet wouldn't have this situation in hand? How do I know anything? Janet has been stronger in her life than I was ever called on to be. She will make sure that Dee is okay and even if she didn't know it, Dee never really needed me at all.

"You know," I say. "People may tell you that this is best time of your life."

"Right," she says.

"It's a lie," I tell her.

"I know," she says.

"Is that boy okay?" I ask. "The one from your school?"

She rolls her eyes. "Of course," she says. "I think so, anyhow."

Dee is the kind of girl you might expect to have nasty little bitten-down stubs for fingernails, but she has long, perfectly-shaped nails. With a real manicure instead of this grunge DIY job her hands would be beautiful—long, slender fingers bare of rings and the colour of skin they must mean when they say *porcelain* on the foundation bottles.

"I think you are going to grow into your hands," I say, surprising even myself.

Dee looks down awkwardly and then holds her hands away from herself as though they are something that should embarrass her. The tips of her ears turn pink.

I reach out to grab her and stop short, my hands hovering above hers. "So lovely," I say. "Like the woman you'll become." And then I give up. "I sound like a tampon ad, don't I?"

She rewards me with a happy snort.

"Okay, fine," I say. "I'll stop. I just wanted to say welcome home."

I would like a bath. Not that I feel unclean, or tired, or too hot or too cold, or any of those other things that used to make me want a bath. It is just that I don't feel anything much at all.

I climb into the bathtub, lying down so that I can look out the skylight. Alec had it cut into the ceiling for me for my birthday one year, with a note saying, *If I could give you the moon . . .*

Then, before I can do anything about it, Janet is in the bathroom with me. Please don't go to the toilet in front of me, I think. But then I realize she is crying. She has the taps running so she can't be heard, and her shoulders are jerking forward like she is trying to fold right into herself. Even with the sound of the tap water babbling I can still hear the sad little gasps she makes between sobs.

I can't be here.

Janet cries like a child. Maybe it's only because she thinks there's no one watching, and this is how everyone cries when they think that they are alone. Maybe I cry this way.

When I sit up straight in the tub I can see her reflection in the vanity mirror. She's not wiping her face clean or trying to hold back the sobs. Her eyes are closed, and her mouth is distorted. It hurts to look at her.

I'm trying to watch as if from a great distance. I am thinking about everything except the fact that I am two feet away from a human being whose all-too-human heart is breaking.

CHAPTER ELEVEN

I SEE ALEC lying on his back in our bed and staring up at me. He looks so sleepy and lovely and warm and rumpled that it makes me want to cry. I seem to be on the ceiling looking down at him. Then I realize that I see myself there in the bed too. I am lying half on top of him with the duvet twisted round my body. My leg is thrown across him, pinning him to the bed. My head is on his shoulder and my face pressed into his pillow. I can imagine that our two hearts are lined up so that together they make one sound. This is the start of the last day.

This is not like the memories I've inhabited because this time I am outside, watching myself like I am a character in a film. And instead of that languid narcotic feeling that comes with memories, now I am filled with a cold, clammy fear.

Alec begins to move, trying to shift out from beneath me. He looks toward the clock on the bedside table and then back to me. He smiles. He is young again. Younger. There is a moment where I could still fit my body to his and keep him with me and change the whole shape of the day, our lives even, perhaps. Instead I watch him ease away and leave the bed, leaving me behind. I sleep on. Wake up, I think. *Fay, wake up.* I roll over in the bed, briefly open my eyes. The sound of the shower starting up in the other room. I close my eyes again.

I could have roused myself. Pulled my weary body from the bed, shaken off the hangover, the laziness, the innate inertia. I could have gone downstairs and made the coffee and it could have been just another ordinary day. Instead, I groan and curl my body into a C. Instead I am here watching myself.

Alec appears in the doorway. He is dressed and ready for work. He stands there a moment looking at me and then comes across and leans in to kiss me.

I mumble at him.

"What's the matter?" he asks.

"Don't kiss me," I say. "I have dragon breath."

He kisses me. Runs his hand under the sheet. Kisses me again. I see it happening rather than feel it. The ache of this.

Alec leaves and I roll over in the bed, turn my head toward the window and the light. The next thing is that my hand comes out of the tangle of sheets and closes on a phone on his bedside table. He's forgotten his phone.

"Alec," I call out.

There is no answer.

I drag myself from the bed. I am wearing only my string of black pearls. I grab the shirt Alec was wearing last night off the chair and pull it around me. There is the sound of the front door slamming shut, and then I run to the window and rap on the glass.

There is something comic in all this pointless activity. Something of the farce. I watch myself run from the room.

Next thing I am at the top of the stairs watching myself tumbling down, arms wildly flailing. I hear the nauseating crack as the back of my skull connects with the wooden stair. And then I am looking down at myself lying there on the floor like a rag doll.

Is that it? I look at myself lying there. Am I dead? Is that what I look like dead?

But then I groan, and I pick myself up off the floor. Look out the window of the front door. I see myself put my hand up to the back of my head, run it over the curve of my skull and then hold it in front of my face. Checking for blood. There is none.

I sit down on the final step to steady myself and then look at the phone in my hand.

Call for help, I think. *Call Alec*. But I have his phone.

After a minute I get up. Stand rubbing the back of my head. Walk out to the kitchen and pour myself a glass of water. Take it into the living room with me. I rub my eyes a few times, the way a child would with scrunched-up fists. I feel absurdly tender watching myself. Unable to do anything. Unable to change what is happening.

I'm standing in the living room looking at the piano. I can't tell what I am thinking as I do this. I watch myself set the half-empty glass down on the coffee table and lie down on the couch, resting my head on the soft velvet of the arm. I turn so that I am gazing at the dollhouse and then I close my eyes.

And that's it.

I look at myself lying there. My body. Is that all I am?

I think about sitting with Marjorie and how from one moment to the next she looked just the same and yet I knew I was alone in the room.

It is all so ordinary. A perfectly ordinary death.

———

Alec is making up his bed in the study for the night. He is humming to himself again and I think about how this is a gift. This little oasis of contentment. The two of us together.

"Alec," I say. He keeps lifting the sheet and letting it fall like a parachute over the couch. I remember him doing this on hot Montreal nights. Me lying naked on the bed and the sheet drifting down over me again and again. "Stop a minute," I say.

He stops. Sits down on the half-made couch. Waits.

I sit beside him. Long to sit closer.

"I hit my head, didn't I?"

"You hit your head," he says. "Yes. I wasn't here."

"I know," I say. "I saw it. Remembered it."

"Not being with you—" His voice breaks.

"It's okay," I say. "You mustn't mind about that."

"Were you afraid?" he asks. "I've always thought you must have been frightened."

"I wasn't," I say.

"I'm glad."

"Alec," I say and am interrupted by a knock at the study door. He looks at me and I stand and walk over to the corner of the room.

"Yes," he says. He clears his throat. "Yes," he says, louder this time, and the door opens. Janet puts her head around the door, and I realize that she is nervous.

"I'm going up now," she says. "Are you sleeping down here again?"

He nods.

Now she steps into the room.

"Al, what is it? What have I done?"

"Nothing. It's nothing. I just won't be good company for you. I have an awful headache." He presses the heels of his hands into the sockets of his eyes. He does look like he is easing a headache, but really I think he is trying not to look at me while he is talking to her.

"Are you all right? Really?" she asks. She kneels down, putting her hands on his thighs and looking up into his face. "Do you think you should see the doctor?"

She is beautiful. It's hard to admit but she really is. There is something so perfectly symmetrical in her features. She has one of those faces that could fill a movie screen. I never looked like that. Not even when I was young. And she is so pure and clean-looking. I'm not even sure she's wearing any makeup at all. I look and her earlobes are perfect and intact. I can't say why, but this is the final insult.

Alec shakes his head. Furrows his brow in a way that signals he is feeling guilty. Stands up and walks in a circle around his desk.

"Janet. I'm sorry. I'm sorry to do this to you." His voice is constrained. I know it isn't because he doesn't feel anything but because he feels too much. I don't know which hurts more.

"If you're sure you're all right," says Janet, uncertainly.

She reaches out for his hands. He doesn't pull away.

"I am," he says, looking into her eyes and trying to smile. "I will be. We'll get through this," he says. And I realize that they will. And that they should.

"Do you think you called me back?" I ask, when she's gone. "Do you think you somehow wished me back into being?"

I wait but he doesn't answer.

"Alec, my love," I say.

"Yes," he says. "Yes, I think that must have been it."

"Tell me about the baby," I say.

"What baby?"

"The one they named for me," I say. "What's she like?"

"I hardly know her," he says. "I've only met her once or twice. Vicki brought her over when she was visiting your mother last Christmas. She brought both girls. They were sweet."

"And . . . ?"

"What do you want me to tell you?" he asks. "She's a baby."

I don't say anything. Wait.

"The thing is, Fay, you would be thrilled to see Vicki now. It's remarkable. It started with the adoption. It was like she opened up . . ." His voice is light. "She is deliriously happy being a mother. Maybe it would have been different if she hadn't waited so long. Tried so hard. But she is so happy."

I picture this. My sister's face. The sweetness in her that had always needed a place to go.

"She has your eyes," he says. "The baby. Fay. She has the look of you." He takes a breath and holds it for an unnaturally long time. "It broke my heart," he says. "It broke my goddamn heart."

I think about that baby. Carrying my name into some future I will have no part of. I think of the baby we lost and all the ones I never had. I told myself for years that what I felt was fear. A fear of failing again. But now I see it for what it really was. An inability to make that decision. To commit to that life. I see that my refusal to take risks limited the life that Alec could have with me, that it was always the unspoken thing between us.

"I think Janet will be able to give you what I couldn't. That makes me almost as happy as it does sad. I know you gave things up because of me. I know you always wanted a family."

"I always thought that if I waited, you'd be ready."

"You don't regret it? Me coming back. All this disruption?" I say disruption when what I mean is pain. All this pain.

"I wouldn't give it up," he says, which is not answering the question but will have to do.

"Remember the Swedenborg?" I ask.

"I do understand now that we are spirits, not bodies," says Alec.

"Why do you think I came back now?" I ask. I see him hesitate. His lips draw tight, as though holding back the words he might say. I release him. "I think it's because you need to move on. I think it's because I want you to have your life. To have someone to share it."

"I'll love you until the day I die," he says. "Longer."

I know. If ever I doubted it, I don't now.

"I'm going to have to go soon," I say.

"Not yet," he says. "Not yet."

CHAPTER TWELVE

IT IS THAT middle bit of the night. Alec lies with his
hands behind his head and looks up at the ceiling. Is he
thinking about his new wife in bed up there? Is he thinking about me and all the nights we lay tangled together?

I sit on the floor beside him. We are perhaps a foot
apart and I think of how in the early days, no matter what
it was that we were doing together, some parts of our
bodies would be in contact. A hand in a hand. A head on
a shoulder. Thigh pressed to thigh.

"Dee thinks she raised me from the dead. She used a
Ouija app on her phone."

"A Ouija app. That's ridiculous."

It's easier to talk to him in this weird half-light. "Completely ridiculous, of course. Except that she called, and I came, and here we are. So." Long silence. I let my eye follow a small maze in the pattern of the rug and wait for Alec to catch up. "She wanted me to ruin your marriage. She wanted her mother to leave you and go back to her first husband. To Dee's father. She wanted her family back."

"That's not going to happen. I told you what he's like. I told you a little of what he's like. That is not going to happen." Alec stands and the blanket falls to the floor. I am happy to see how moved he is by this. "We're her family now. She's safe here."

"Good," I say. "I want her to be safe. I really, really, want that. She was cutting herself, Alec. Self-harming."

"Yes, we know all about that. Janet's taking her to see someone. She's doing better. We're keeping an eye on her. Trying to get her to spend more time with the living."

Our eyes meet. I have to laugh. "I'm serious, Alec. I want her to be loved. I want her to be cherished and adored and all of those things that our child—if we'd had one—would have been."

Alec sits back down on the side of the couch, cradles his hands behind his head and leans forward.

I lie down on the floor beside him and cross my arms over my chest. Are people in coffins really laid out that way, or is that just on stone effigies? I roll over onto my side and prop my head up on my hand.

"I want you to have your family, Alec. I want everything for you."

"I had so many things I wanted to tell you. Something would happen and I would think, 'I can't wait to tell Fay,' but then I couldn't. It meant that for a long time nothing felt real. That anything I couldn't share with you hadn't really happened, in a sense. I felt like I was living a pretend life."

"And then what?"

He looks guilty. Rubs his hands over his face as though he is trying to erase something from his expression.

"Life is an irresistible force. Like all you want to do is stand still and you keep on getting pulled forward. So I had to get up every day and shave my face and put on clothes and talk to people and pretend to be one of the living. And I guess after a while I forgot I was pretending. And then eventually I started just living again."

"That's nothing to be ashamed of," I say. But a small part of me still thinks *how could he?* How could he live when I was dead? How could he eat a sandwich or watch a movie or kiss another woman? Love another woman. "I can't say what I would have done if it was me." I can't say but I know. I would have died too.

"It's like I'm walking around with an arrow in my heart, Fay. I don't always feel it but it's always there. And something—some little unguarded movement—can make the pain just as sharp and brutal as it was that first day."

He looks at me to see if I understand. I do. I think I do.

"It's time to stop this," I say. "You can't sleep here tonight, my love. This isn't where you belong."

I pick up his mohair blanket and put it inside the cupboard, pushing the door firmly closed. Without saying anything more he stands and blindly stumbles out of the room. I hear his footfall on the stairs and then a door opening at the top.

Morning. I know now that it is time for me to go for good. Time for me to let Alec go.

But still, I can't leave without saying goodbye to Dee. I find her down in the cellar pushing things into a backpack.

"I have to go," she says.

"So do I," I say. "Are you going to be okay?"

She looks up at me, her gaze briefly more direct than it has been before. "Mom said that I am more important to her than anything. Do you think that's true?"

The one thing that everyone always wants to hear from the person they love.

"Of course it is," I say.

I follow her to the front door. Watch as she pulls on a pair of leopard-printed sneakers.

She is a totally different person—the goth girl, the cutter has been left behind. She is cycling through personas and waiting to choose one. This too will pass.

"I'm leaving for good this time."

"Yeah," she says.

I move to stand in front of her. She looks out the window. She is deliberately avoiding looking at me.

"Alec is a good man—" I begin, then stop and begin again: "Your mother has been through a lot. She deserves to be happy. You all do."

"I've got to go out now," she says brusquely. She glances up and for the first time I see Janet in her face.

"Of course," I say. "Goodbye."

She's fine. If she's not then she will be. She has Alec. She has her mother. And then she goes, just like that. I'm glad that she doesn't need me. I'm glad she has what she needs.

I look out the window and see her stalking down the street. Her pale hair electric on her head. My not-ghost girl. I'd half hoped to see someone out there waiting for her, but she is alone. The only good thing about being thirteen is that unlike being dead, it doesn't last.

I find Alec in his study. He is looking out the window and when I say his name he turns to me and smiles and the look he gives me is everything I didn't know I needed.

"I just said goodbye to Dee. It's like she's turning into a different person," I say.

"They do that," he says. "At this age. She's figuring out who she is. Who she wants to be."

The children we never had feel near to me. Not in the room with us but not so far away either.

"Alec," I say. "I'm frightened."

"What are you afraid of?" he asks.

"Everything," I say. "I'm afraid of being forgotten," I say before I even know I am going to say it.

"That's not going to happen," he says.

Replaced is not forgotten, I tell myself. Replaced is you leaving such a void behind you in the world that if it is not filled in some way then everything—absolutely everything—will fall into it. I look at him and know this to be true.

I am weary. I don't recall ever being this weary. I sit down on the floor and then go right ahead and lie down, stretching myself out on the beautiful carpet.

Alec looks at me there for a moment and then lies down beside me. We are parallel lines that never touch. So much has changed in the time that I've been away. So much has changed since I've been back. All I wanted is what I have right here in this room.

"Do you think things happen for a reason?" I ask.

"Oh," says Alec. "That's the big question, isn't it?"

"That's not an answer," I say.

"I do believe," he says. "I do believe it now . . ."

"Why now?"

"Because you died. That's a thing that happened. I don't know why it happened—haven't the faintest idea—but if I believe, as I did for a long time, that it was random, then I'll go mad. I would do anything to live in a world where it hadn't happened, but that world is gone, lost to me. I have to live in this one."

"I feel like I am slipping away," I say.

"I know," he says.

"I suppose it was all borrowed time, wasn't it? Being here with you. This wasn't supposed to happen and somehow it did. I should be grateful."

"It was never going to be enough," he says.

I am thinking about Swedenborg. About the book Alec was reading on the day we met. About his face as he looked up at me for the first time. "It was, though. It was enough."

And then we just lie side by side and are quiet for the longest time.

"I'm going to have to go soon," I say finally.

"Not yet," says Alec.

"You look . . ." I pause, and try to smile. "You look tired." I was going to say old. He does look old. And he will get older still.

"You have to understand," he says slowly. "While you were alive, I only ever wanted to be married to you."

"Okay," I say. And then, more kindly: "I know."

"When you died—when I lost you—it was like I was handed this heavy stone. And I had to carry it everywhere I went. And the stone doesn't diminish over time. It never gets lighter. It just gets to feel normal to be carrying it with you everywhere you go."

"I had the easy job, didn't I?" I say.

And then neither of us says anything for a long time.

Finally, I say to him: "I'm reaching out and taking you by the hand."

At first it is as dark as it has ever been. And then slowly the outlines of the objects in the room appear, like a developing photograph.

As the image begins to come clear, I see that the room is blindingly white. I am lying on a metal bed with rails on the sides. There are tubes running into me and out of me. I can see my chest rise and fall. I wonder if I am dreaming.

I hear some mechanical sound from the distant nearby. A machine. "Don't go," Alec says. "Don't leave me yet." His voice comes to me disembodied, although I am the one leaving my body behind.

I let myself fall back into my body. My body and yet not my body. Strangely different. I hold my firstborn in my arms and nuzzle his downy baby head. His tiny fist unfurls against my breast and as he suckles his eyes never leave mine. I feel bonded to him, as I never have to another human being. Everywhere his skin touches mine it is like I could almost reabsorb him, and we could be one again. The tug of him on my breast runs straight through the core of me to my womb and I feel anchored and solid and powerful. This is bliss.

And then it is over.

I open my eyes and see that everything is back to the way I left it on my last day. I lie down on top of the silk duvet on my beautiful bed. Alec's and my bed. The word *home* pops into my head. I close my eyes.

I can hear a beeping or alarm. A horn blaring? Insistent.

When I open my eyes again, I am lying on the floor with Alec's coat beneath me and several sweaters spread over me. I run my hands over their textures and think, *oh, this is the first day.* The bright light is spilling through the uncurtained windows. Time stands still and the house travels through it.

The sound outside is the truck with all of our things that have followed us across the country, and in a moment I will wake properly. I will go down the stairs and open the door and let them in and Alec and I will begin our life together here.

And then I remember.

I must go.

Alec is standing in the entranceway looking out at the street through the pane of glass in the front door. And although I can't see his face, I know that he is weeping. I know it from the set of his shoulders and the tremor that runs through the back of his dear, sweet neck.

I raise my hand but stop short of touching him. He turns and I see how this is stealing the breath from him.

I turn the deadbolt for the last time and pull open the door. Outside there is nothing but light. Is white the absence of colour or all colours at once? Funny how I can't remember.

The noise I was hearing stops abruptly. The silence is immaculate.

Alec holds on to the doorframe as though he is in danger of falling. I want to speak to him but can't. It doesn't matter. There's nothing to say that I haven't already told him.

I look into his face one last time to be sure, and then I step through the open door.

ACKNOWLEDGEMENTS

If I thanked everyone who has helped me along the way the pages would outnumber those of my story.

My family and friends have been my support throughout the writing of this book, and I can never express how grateful I am for that and for so much else.

My mother, June McDonald, taught me to read, to write, and to love. There would be no book without her.

My husband, Daniel O'Leary, has seen me through years of stumbling along in the dark following my ghost and his love and constancy is what sustained me.

My children were a dream that came true for me and I am so grateful that they are in the world.

Jackie Kaiser of Westwood Creative has been the best of agents and the truest of friends to both me and this book.

Martha Kanya-Forstner is a dream of an editor, one who saw this story for what it could be.

SARA O'LEARY is a writer of fiction for both adults and children. She is the author of a collection of short stories, *Comfort Me With Apples*; a series of postcard stories, *Wish You Were Here*; and a number of critically acclaimed picture books, including *This Is Sadie*, which was adapted for the stage by the New York City Children's Theater.